SHOWDOWN AT YELLOW BUTTE

Louis L'Amour

FAWCETT GOLD MEDAL • NEW YORK

TO YALE

SHOWDOWN AT YELLOW BUTTE

This book was originally published under the pseudonym "Jim Mayo."

Published by Fawcett Gold Medal Books, a unit of CBS Publications, the Consumer Publishing Division of CBS Inc., by arrangement with the author.

ISBN: 0-449-14275-2

Printed in the United States of America.

First Fawcett printing: November 1974

23   22   21   20   19   18   17   16   15

CHAPTER I

EVERYTHING was quiet in Mustang. Three whole days had passed without a killing. The townfolk, knowing their community, were not fooled. They had long since resigned themselves to the inevitable. In fact, they would be relieved when the situation was back to normal—a killing every day; more on hot days. Several days without deadly gun play built up a mounting tension that was unbearable. Who would be next?

Moreover, with Clay Allison, who had killed thirty men, playing poker over at the Morrison House, and Black Jack Ketchum, who richly deserved the hanging he was soon to get, sleeping off a drunk at the St. James—trouble could be expected in the very near future.

The walk before the St. James was now cool, and Captain Tom Kedrick, a stranger in town, sat in a well-polished chair and studied the street with interested eyes.

He was a tall young man with rusty brown hair and green eyes, quiet mannered and quick to smile. Women never failed to look twice, and when their eyes met his their hearts pounded, a fact of which

Tom Kedrick was totally unaware. He knew women seemed to like him, but it never failed to leave him mildly astonished.

The street he watched was crowded with buckboards, freight wagons, a newly arrived stage and one about to depart. All the hitch-rails were lined with saddled horses wearing a variety of brands.

Kedrick, suddenly aware that a young man stood beside him, glanced up. The fellow was scarcely more than a boy and he had soft brown eyes and hair that needed cutting. "Cap'n Kedrick?" he inquired. "John Gunter sent me. I'm Dornie Shaw."

"Oh, yes!" Kedrick got to his feet, smiling, and thrust out his hand. "Nice to know you, Shaw. Are you working for Gunter?"

Shaw's brown eyes were faintly ironic. "With him," he corrected. "I work for no man."

"I see."

Kedrick did not see at all, but he was prepared to wait and find out. There was something oddly disturbing about this young man, something that had Kedrick on edge and queerly alert. "Where's Gunter now?"

"Down the street. He asked me to check an' see if you were here, an' if you were, to ask you to stick around close to the hotel. He'll be along soon."

"All right. Sit down, why don't you?"

Shaw glanced briefly at the chairs. "I'll stand. I never sit in no chair with arms on them. Apt to get in the way."

"In the way?" Kedrick glanced up, and then his eyes fell to the two guns Shaw wore, their butts hanging wide. "Oh, yes! I see." He nodded at the guns. "The town marshal doesn't object?"

Dornie Shaw looked at him, smiling slowly. "Not

6

to me, he don't. Wouldn't do him no good if he did."

"Anyway," he added after a minute, "not in Mustang. Too many hard cases. I never seen a marshal could make it stick in this town."

Kedrick smiled. "Hickok? Earp? Masterson?"

"Maybe," Dornie Shaw was openly skeptical, "but I doubt it. Allison's here. So's Ketchum. Billy the Kid's been around, and some of that crowd. A marshal in this town would have to be mighty fast, an' prove it ever' day."

"Maybe you're right." He studied Shaw surreptitiously. What was it about him that was so disturbing? Not the two guns, for he had seen many men who wore guns, had been reared among them, in fact. No, it was something else, some quality he could not define, but it was a sort of lurking menace, an odd feeling about such a calm-eyed young man.

"We've got some good men," Shaw volunteered, after a minute. "Picked up a couple today. Laredo Shad's goin' to be one of the best, I'm thinkin'. He's a tough hand, an' gun wise as all get out. Three more come in today. Fessenden, Poinsett an' Goff."

Obviously, from the manner in which he spoke, the names meant much to Shaw, but they meant exactly nothing to Kedrick. Fessenden seemed to strike some sort of a responsive note but he could not put a finger on it. His eyes strayed down the street, studying the crowd. "You think they'll really fight?" he asked, studying the street. "Are there enough of them?"

"That bunch?" Shaw's voice was dry. "They'll fight, all right. You got some tough boys in that outfit. Injun scrappers, an' such like. They won't

7

scare worth a durn." He glanced curiously at Kedrick. "Gunter says you're a fighter."

Was that doubt in Shaw's voice? Kedrick smiled, then shrugged. "I get along. I was in the Army, if that means anything."

"Been West before?"

"Sure! I was born in California, just before the Rush. When the war broke out I was sixteen, but I went in with a bunch from Nevada. Stayed in a couple of years after the war, fighting Apaches!"

Shaw nodded, as if satisfied. "Gunter thinks well of you, but he's only one of them, an' not the most important one."

A short, thick-set man with a square-cut beard, that made him look enough like General Grant to be his twin, was pushing through the crowd toward them. He even smoked a thick black cigar.

The man walking beside him was tall as Kedrick, who stood an easy inch above six feet. He had a sharply cut face and his eyes were cold, but they were the eyes of a man born to command, a man who could be utterly ruthless. That would be Colonel Loren Keith. That meant there was still one left he had to meet—Burwick. The three were partners, and of the three, only Burwick was from the area.

Gunter smiled quickly, his lips parting over clenched white teeth that gripped his cigar. He thrust out his hand. "Good to see you, Kedrick! Colonel, this is our man! If there ever was a man born to ramrod this thing through, this is the one! I told you of that drive he made for Patterson! Took those cattle through without losing a head, rustlers an' Comanches be danged!"

Keith nodded, his cold eyes taking in Kedrick at

8

a glance. "Captain—that was an army title, Kedrick?"

"Army. The War Between the States."

"I see. There was a Thomas Kedrick who was a sergeant in the fighting against the Apaches."

"That was me. All of us went down some in rank after the troops were discharged."

"How much time in the war?" Keith's eyes still studied him.

"Four years, and two campaigning in the Southwest."

"Not bad. You should know what to expect in a fight." His eyes went to Kedrick's, faintly mocking. "I have twelve years, myself. Regular army."

Kedrick found that Keith's attitude irritated him. He meant to say nothing, but suddenly he was speaking. "My American army experience, Colonel, was only part of the story. I was with Bazaine, at the defense of Metz, in the Franco-Prussian War. I escaped, and was with MacMahon at the Battle of Sedan."

Keith's eyes sharpened and his lips thinned. Kedrick could feel the sharp dislike rising in the man.

"Is that all?" he asked coolly.

"Why, no. Since you ask, it was not. I was with Wolseley, in the Second Ashanti War, in Africa. And I was in the two-year campaign against the Tungans of northern T'ien Shan—with the rank of General."

"You seem to get around a good bit," Keith said dryly, " a genuine mercenary!"

Kedrick smiled, undisturbed. "If you like. That's what you want here, isn't it? Men who can fight? Isn't it customary for some men to hire others to do their fighting for them?"

9

Colonel Keith's face flamed, then went white, but before he could speak, a big, square-faced man thrust himself through the crowd and stopped to face them.

"You, is it, Gunter?" the man cried. "Well, I've heard tell the reason why you're here, an' if you expect to take from hard-workin' men the land they've slaved for, you better come a-shootin'!"

Before anyone could speak, Dornie slid between Keith and Gunter and fronted the man. "You lookin' for trouble? You want to start your shootin' now?"

His voice was low, almost a purr, but Kedrick was startled by the shocked expression on the man's face. He drew back, holding his hands wide. "I wasn't bracin' you, Dornie! Didn't even know you was around!"

"Then get out!" Dornie Shaw snarled, passion suddenly breaking through his calmness, passion, and something else, something Kedrick spotted with a shock—the driving urge to kill!

"Get out!" Shaw repeated. "An' if you want to live, keep goin'!"

Stumblingly, the man turned and ducked into the hastily assembled crowd, and Tom Kedrick, scanning their faces, found hard indifference there, or hatred. In no face did he see warmth or friendly feeling. He frowned thoughtfully, then turned away.

Gunter caught his arm, eager to take advantage of the break the interruption had made to bring peace between the two. "You see what we're up against?" he began. "Now that was Peters. He's harmless, but there's others would have drawn, and drawn fast! They won't be all like that! Let's go meet Burwick!"

Kedrick fell in beside Gunter, who carefully interposed himself between the two men. Once, Tom glanced back. What had become of Dornie Shaw he did not know, but he did know that Dornie, who was to be his second in command, was a killer. He knew the type from of old.

Yet he was disturbed more than he cared to admit by the man who had challenged them. Peters had the look of an honest man, even if not an intelligent one. Of course, there might be honest men among them, if they were men of Peters' stripe. But Peters seemed to be a follower, and he might follow where the wrong men led.

Certainly, if this land was going to Gunter, Keith and Burwick through a Government bill, there could be nothing wrong with the deal. If the Government sold the land to them, squatters had no rights on it. Still, if there were many like Peters the job was not going to be all he had expected.

Gunter stopped before a square stone house set back from the street. "This here's headquarters," he said. "We hole up here when in town. Come on in."

A wide veranda skirted the house, and as they stepped upon it they saw a girl in a gray skirt and white blouse sitting a few feet away with an open book in her lap. Gunter halted.

"Cap'n Kedrick, my niece, Consuelo Duane."

Their eyes met—and held. For a breathless moment no voice was lifted. Tom Kedrick felt as though his muscles had gone dead, for he could not move. Her own eyes were wide, startled.

Kedrick recovered himself with a start. He bowed.

"Miss Duane!"

"Captain Kedrick," somehow she was on her feet and moving toward him, "I hope you'll like it here!"

His eyes had not left hers, and now color was coming into her cheeks. "I shall!" he said gently. "Nothing can prevent me now."

"Don't be too sure of that, Captain!" Keith's voice was sharp and cold. "We are late for our visit. Let's be going. Your pardon, Connie. Burwick is waiting."

Kedrick glanced back as he went through the door, and the girl was still standing there, poised, motionless.

Keith's irritation was obvious, but Gunter seemed to have noticed nothing. Dornie Shaw, who had materialized from somewhere, glanced briefly at Kedrick, but said no word. Coolly, he began to roll a smoke.

CHAPTER II

BURWICK crouched behind a table. He was an incredibly fat man, and unbelievably dirty. A stubble of graying beard covered his jowls and his several chins, yet the eyes that measured Kedrick from beneath the almost hairless brows were sharp, malignant, and set close alongside a nose too small for his face. His shirt was open, and the edge of the collar was greasy. Rims of black marked each fingernail.

He glanced at the others, then back at Kedrick. "Sit down!" he said. "You're late! Business won't wait!" His bulbous head swung from Kedrick to Gunter. "John, this the man who'll ramrod those skunks off that land? This him?"

"Yes, that's Kedrick," Gunter said hastily. Oddly enough, he seemed almost frightened of Burwick. Keith had said nothing since they entered the room. Quietly, he seemed to have withdrawn, stepped momentarily from the picture. It was, Kedrick was to discover, a faculty he had when Burwick was near. "He'll do the job, all right!"

Burwick turned his eyes on Kedrick after a moment. He nodded. "Know a good deal about you, son!" His voice was almost genial. "You'll do if you don't get soft with them! We've no time to waste, you understand! They've had notice to move. Give 'em one more notice, then get 'em off or bury 'em. That's your business, not mine. I'll ask no questions," he added sharply, "an' I'll see nobody else does. What happens here is our business."

He dismissed Kedrick from his mind and turned his attention to Gunter. "You've ordered like I told you? Grub for fifty men for fifty days? Once this situation is cleaned up I want to get busy at once. The sooner we have work started, the sooner we'll be all set. I want no backfiring on this job."

Burwick turned sharply at Tom Kedrick. "Ten days! I give you ten days! If you need more than five I'll be disappointed. If you've not the heart for it, turn Dornie loose. Dornie'll show 'em." He cackled suddenly. "That's right. Dornie'll show 'em!"

He sobered down, glanced at the papers on his desk, then without looking up, "Kedrick, you can go. Dornie, you run along, too!"

13

Kedrick hesitated, then arose. "How many of these men are there?" he asked suddenly. "Have any of them families?"

Gunter turned on him nervously. "I'll tell you all you need to know, Tom. See you later!"

Kedrick shrugged, and picking up his hat, walked out. Dornie Shaw had already vanished. When he reached the veranda, Connie Duane still sat there. She was staring over the top of her book at the dusty, sun-swept street.

He paused, hat in hand. "Have you been in Mustang long?"

She looked up, studying him for a long minute before she spoke. "Why, no. Not long. Yet long enough to learn to love and hate." She turned her eyes to the hills, then back to him. "I love this country, Captain. Can you understand that?

"I'm a city girl, born and bred in the city, and yet when I first saw those red rock walls, those lonely mesas, the desert, the Indian ponies—why, Captain, I fell in love! This is my country. I could stay here forever."

Surprised, he studied her again, more pleased than he could easily have admitted. "That's the way I feel about it. But you said to love and to hate. You love the country. Now what do you hate?"

"Some of the men who infest it, Captain. Some of the human wolves it breeds, and others, bred elsewhere, who come to it to feed off the ones who came earlier and were more courageous but are less knowing, less tricky."

More and more surprised, he leaned on the rail. "I don't know if I follow you, Miss Duane. I haven't been here long, but I haven't met any of those you speak of."

14

She looked up at him, her eyes frank and cool. Slowly, she closed her book and turned toward the door. "You haven't, Captain?" Her voice was suddenly cool. "Are you sure? At this moment, I am wondering if you are not one of them!" She stepped thought the door and was gone.

Tom Kedrick stood for a moment, staring after her. When he turned away it was with a puzzled frown on his face. Now what did she mean by that? What did she know about him that could incline her to such a view? Despite himself, he was both irritated and disturbed. Coupled with the anger of the man Peters, it offered a new element to his thinking. Yet, how could Consuelo Duane, John Gunter's niece, have the same opinion owned by Peters? No doubt they stemmed from different sources.

Troubled, he walked on down to the street of the town and stood there, looking around.

He had not yet changed into Western clothes, and wore a flat-crowned, flat-brimmed black hat, which he would retain, a tailored gray suit, and black Western-style boots. Pausing on the corner, he slowly rolled a cigarette and lighted it. He made a dashing, handsome figure as he stood there in his perfectly fitted suit, his lean, bronzed face strong, intelligent, and alert.

Both men and women glanced at him and most of them looked twice. His military erectness, broad shoulders and cool self-possession were enough to mark him in any crowd. His mind had escaped his immediate problem now and was lost in the never-ending excitement of a crowded Western street. All kinds of men and women seemed jammed together without rhyme or reason.

For the West was of all things, a melting pot. Adventurers came to seek gold, new lands, excitement. Gamblers, women of the oldest and most active profession, thugs, gunmen, cow rustlers, horsethieves, miners, cowhands, freighters and just drifters—all crowded the street. That bearded unshaven man in the sun-faded red wool shirt might, if prompted, start to spout Shakespeare. The slender young man talking to the girl in the buckboard might have graduated from Oxford, and the white-faced gambler might be the scion of an old Southern family.

All men wore guns, most of them in plain sight. Few of them would hesitate to use them if need be. The man who fought with his fists, although present, was a rarity.

A big man lurched from the crowd. Tom glanced at him, and their eyes met. Obviously, the man had been drinking and was hunting trouble. In Kedrick, he thought he found it. Sensing a fight, other passers-by became wary and stopped to watch.

"So?" The big man stood wide legged, his sleeves rolled about thick, hairy forearms. " 'Nother one of them durn thieves! Land stealers!" He chuckled suddenly. "Well, your murderer ain't with you now to save your bacon, an' I aim to git my share of you right now! Reach!"

Kedrick's mouth was dry, but his eyes were calm. He held the cigarette in his right hand near his mouth. "Sorry, friend. I'm not packing a gun. If I were, I'd still not kill you. You're mistaken, man, about that land. My people have a rightful claim to it."

"Have they, now?" The big man came a step nearer, his hand on the butt of his gun. "The right to take from a man the land he's sweated over? To tear down his home? To run his kids out on the desert?"

Despite the fact that the man was drunk, Tom Kedrick saw beyond it a sullen and honest fury—and fear. Not fear for him, for this man was not afraid, nor would he be afraid of Dornie Shaw. He was afraid for his family. The realization of that fact struck Kedrick and disturbed him anew. More and more he was questioning the course he had chosen.

The crowd murmured and was ugly. Obviously, their sympathies were with the big man, and against Kedrick.

A low murmur, then a rustling in the crowd, and suddenly: deathly silence. Kedrick saw the big man's face pale, and heard someone whisper hoarsely, "Look out, Burt! It's Dornie Shaw!"

Kedrick was suddenly aware that Shaw had moved up beside him. "Let me have him, Cap'n," Shaw's voice was low. "It's time this here was stopped."

Kedrick's voice was sharp, cold. "No! Move back, Shaw! I'll fight my own battles!"

"But you ain't got a gun!" Shaw's voice was sharper in protest.

Burt showed no desire to retreat. That the appearance of Shaw had shocked him was evident, but this man was not Peters. He was going to stand his ground. His eyes, wary now, but puzzled, shifted from Shaw to Kedrick, and Tom took an easy step forward, putting himself almost within arm's length of Burt.

"Shaw's not in this, Burt," he said quietly. "I've no quarrel with you, man, but no man calls me without getting his chance. If you want what I've

17

got, don't let the fact that I'm not armed stop you. I wanted no quarrel, but you do—so have at it!"

Suspicion was in the big man's eyes. He had seen guns come from nowhere before, and especially from men dressed as this one. He was not prepared to believe that Kedrick would face him unarmed. "You got a gun!" he snapped. "You got a hide-out, you durned coyote!"

He jerked his gun from the holster and in that instant, Tom Kedrick moved. The edge of his left hand chopped down on the rising wrist of the gun-hand, and he stepped in, whipping up his right in an uppercut that packed all the power in his lean, whipcord body. The punch was fast and perfectly timed, and the crack of it on the corner of Burt's jaw was like the snap of a teamster's whip. Burt hit the walk just one split second after his gun, and he hit it right on his shoulder blades.

Coolly then, Kedrick stooped and picked up the gun, an old 1851 Model Navy revolver. He stood over the man, his eyes searching the crowd. Wherever he looked there were hard, blank faces. He glanced down at Burt. The big man was slowly sitting up, shaking his big head. He started to lift his right hand, and gave a sudden gasp of pain. He stared at it, then looked up. "You broke my wrist!" he said. "It's busted! An' me with my plowin' to do!"

"Better get up," Kedrick said quietly. "You asked for it, you know."

When the man was on his feet, Kedrick calmly handed him his six-shooter. Their eyes met over the gun and Kedrick smiled. "Take it. Drop it down in your holster an' forget it. I'm not worried. You're not the man to shoot another in the back."

Calmly, he turned his back and walked slowly

18

away down the street. Before the St. James, he paused. His fingers trembled ever so slightly as he took out a paper and shook tobacco into it.

"That was slick." It was Dornie Shaw's soft voice. His brown eyes probed Kedrick's face curiously. "Never seen the like! Just slapped his wrist an' busted it!"

With Keith, John Gunter had also come up, and he was smiling broadly. "Saw it all, son! That'll do more good than a dozen killings! Just like Tom Smith used to do! Old Bear Creek Tom who handled some of the toughest rannies that ever came over the trail with nothin' but his fists!"

"What would you have done if he had jerked that gun back and fired?" Keith asked.

Kedrick shrugged, wanting to forget it. "He hadn't time," he said quietly. "But there are answers to that, too!"

"Some of the boys will be up to see you tonight, Tom," Gunter advised. "I've had Dornie notify Shad, Fessenden and some of the others. Better figure on a ride out there tomorrow. Makin' a start, anyway. Just sort of ride around with some of the boys to let 'em know we ain't foolin'."

Kedrick nodded, and after a brief discussion went inside and to his room. Certainly, he reflected, the West had not changed. Things still happened fast out here.

He pulled off his coat, waistcoat and vest, then his boots. Stripped to the waist, he sat down on the bed and dug into his valise. For a couple of minutes he dug around and then drew out two well-oiled holsters and gun belts. In the holsters were two .44 Russian pistols, a Smith & Wesson gun, manufactured on order for the Russian Army, and one of the most accurate shooting pistols on the market up to that time.

Carefully, he checked the loads, then returned the guns to their holsters and put them aside. Digging around, he drew out a second pair of guns, holsters and belts. Each of these was a Walch twelve-shot Navy pistol, caliber .36, and almost identical in size and weight to the Frontier Colt or the .44 Russian.

Rarely seen in the West, and disliked by some, Kedrick had used the guns on many occasions and found them always satisfactory. There were times when the added fire power was a big help. As for stopping power, the .36 in the hands of a good marksman lacked but little that offered by the heavier .44 caliber.

Yet, there was a time and a place for everything, and these guns had an added tactical value. Carefully, he wrapped them once more and returned them to the bottom of his valise. Then he belted on the .44 Russians, and digging out his Winchester, carefully cleaned, oiled and loaded it. Then he sat down on the bed and was about to remove his guns again and stretch out, when there was a light tap at the door.

"Come in," said Kedrick, "and if you're an enemy, I'll be pleased to know you!"

The door opened and closed all in a breath. The man that stood with his back to it facing Kedrick was scarcely five-feet-four, yet almost as broad as he was tall. All of him seemed the sheer power of bone and muscle, and not an ounce of fat anywhere. His broad brown face might have been graved from stone, and the bristle of shortcropped hair above it was black as a crow's wing. The man's neck spread to broad, thick shoulders. On his right hip he packed a gun. In his hand he held a narrow-brimmed hard hat.

Kedrick leaped to his feet. "Dai!" The name was an explosion of sound. "Dai Reid! What are you doing in this country?"

"Ah? So it's that you ask, is it? Well, it's trouble there is, much of trouble! An' you that's by way of bringin' it!"

"Me?" Kedrick waved to a chair. "Tell me what you mean."

The Welshman searched his face, then seated himself, his huge palms resting on his knees. His legs were thick muscled and bowed. "It's the man Burwick you're with? An' you've the job taken to run us off the land? There is changed you are, Tom, an' for the worse!"

"You're one of them? You're on the land Burwick, Keith and Guiter claim?"

"I am that. And a sight of work I've done on it, too. An' now the rascals would be puttin' me off. Well, they'll have a fight to move me—an' you, too, Tom Kedrick, if you're to stay one of them."

Kedrick studied the Welshman thoughtfully. All his doubts had come to a head now . . . for this man, he knew. His own father had been Welsh, his mother Irish, and Dai Reid had been friend to them both. Dai had come from the old country with his father, had worked beside him when he courted his mother, and although much younger than Gwilym Kedrick, he had come West with him, too.

"Dai," he said slowly, "I'll admit that today I've been having doubts of all this. You see, I knew John Gunter after the war, and I took a herd of cattle over the trail for a friend of his. There was trouble that year, the Indians holding up every herd and demanding large numbers of cattle for themselves, the rustlers trying to steal whole herds, and others demanding money for passage across land they claimed. I took my herd through without paying anything but a few fat beefs for the Indians, who richly deserved them. But not what they demanded —they got what I wanted to give.

"Gunter remembered me from that, and knew something of my war record, so when he approached me in New Orleans, his proposition sounded good. And this is what he told me.

"His firm, Burwick, Keith and Gunter, had filed application for the survey and purchase of all or parts of nearly three hundred sections of land. They made oath that this land was swampland, or overflowed and came under the General Land Office ruling that it was 'land too wet for irrigation at seeding time, though later requiring irrigation, and thefore subject to sale as swamp.'

"He went on to say that they had arranged to buy the land, but that a bunch of squatters were on it who refused to leave. He wanted to hire me to lead a force to see the land was cleared, and he said that most of them were rustlers, outlaws or renegades of one sort or another. There would be fighting and force would be necessary."

Dai nodded. "Right he was as to the fighting, but renegades, no. Well," he smiled grimly past his pipe. "I'd not be saying that now, but there's mighty few. There are bad apples in all barrels, one or two," he said. "But most of us be good people, with homes built and crops in.

"An' did he tell you that their oath was given that the land was unoccupied? Well, it was! And

22

let me tell you. Ninety-four sections have homes on them, some mighty poor, but homes.

"Shrewd they were with the planning. Six months the notices must be posted, but they posted them in fine print and where few men would read, and three months are by before anything is noticed, and by accident only. So now they come to force us off, to be sure the land is unoccupied and ready. As for swamp, 'tis desert now, and always desert. Crops can only be grown where the water is, an' little enough of that."

Dai shook his head and knocked out his short-stemmed pipe. "Money we've none to fight them, no lawyers among us, although one who's as likely to help, a newspaper man, he is. But what good without money to send him to Washington?"

The Welshman's face was gloomy. "They'll beat us, that we know. They've money to fight us with, and tough men. But some of them will die on the ground, and pay for it with their red blood. And those among us there are who plan to see 'tis not only the hired gunners who die, but the high an' mighty. You, too, lad, if among them you stay."

Kedrick was thoughtful. "Dai, this story is different from the one I've had. I'll have to think about it, and tomorrow we ride out to look the land over and show ourselves."

Reid looked up sharply. "Don't you be one of them, bye! We've plans made to see no man gets off alive if we can help it."

"Look, man!" Kedrick leaned forward. "You've got to change that! I mean, for now. Tomorrow it's mainly a show of force, a threat. There will be no shooting, I promise you. We'll ride out, look around, then ride back. If there's shooting, your men will

23

start it. Now you go back to them and stop it. Let them hold off, and let me look around."

Dai Reid got slowly to his feet. "Ah, lad! 'tis good to see you again, but under happier circumstances I wish it were! I'd have you to the house for supper and a game, as in the old days! You'd like the wife I have!"

"You? Married?" Kedrick was incredulous. "I'd never believe it!"

Dai grinned sheepishly. "Married it is, all right, and happy, Tom." His face darkened. "Happy if I can keep my ground. But one promise I make! If your bloody riders take my ground, my body will be there when they ride past, and it will be not alone, but with dead men around!"

Long after the Welshman had gone, Tom Kedrick sat silently and studied the street below the window. Was this what Consuelo Duane had meant? Whose side was she on? First, he must ride over the land, see it for himself, and then he must have another talk with Gunter. Uneasily, he looked again at the faces of the men in his mind. The cold, wolf-like face of Keith; the fat, slobby face of Burwick, underlined with harsh, domineering power; and the face of Gunter, friendly, affable, but was it not a little . . . sly?

From outside came the noise of a tinny piano, and a strident female voice, singing. Chips rattled, and there was the constant rustle of movement and of booted feet. Somewhere a spur jingled, and Tom Kedrick got to his feet and slipped into a shirt. When he was dressed again, with his guns belted on, he left his room and walked down the hall to the lobby.

24

From a room beside him, a man stepped and stared after him. It was Dornie Shaw.

CHAPTER III

ONLY the dweller in the deserts can know such mornings, such silences, drowsy with warmth and the song of the cicadas. Nowhere but in the desert do the far miles stand out so clearly, the mesas, towers and cliffs so boldly outlined. Nowhere will the cloud shadows island themselves upon the desert, offering their brief respite from the sun.

Six riders, their saddles creaking, six hard men, each lost in the twisted arroyos of his own thoughts, were emerging upon the broad desert. They were men who rode with guns, men who had used their guns to kill and would use them so again. Some of them were already doomed by the relentless and ruthless tide of events; and to the others their time, too, would come.

Each of them was alone, as men who live by the gun are always alone. To them, each man was a potential enemy, each shadow a danger. They rode jealously, their gestures marked by restraint, their eyes by watchfulness.

A horse blew through his nostrils, a hoof clicked

on a stone, someone shifted in his saddle and sighed. These were the only sounds. Tom Kedrick rode an appaloosa gelding, fifteen hands even, with iron-gray forequarters and starkly white hindquarters splashed with tear-shaped spots of black—a clean-limbed horse, strong and fast, with quick, intelligent eyes and interested ears.

When they bunched to start their ride, Laredo Shad stopped to stare at the horse, walking around it admiringly. "You're lucky, friend. That's a horse! Where'd you find him?"

"Navajo remuda. He's a Nez Perce war horse, a long ways off his reservation."

Kedrick noticed the men as they gathered and how they all sized him up carefully, noting his Western garb, and especially, the low-hung, tied-down guns. Yesterday, they had seen him in the store clothes he had worn from New Orleans, but now they could size him up better, judge him with their own kind.

He was tall and straight, and of his yesterday's clothing only the black, flat-crowned hat remained, the hat, and the high-heeled rider's boots. He wore a gray wool shirt now and a black silk kerchief around his neck. His jeans were black, and the two guns rode easily in position, ready for the swing of his hand.

Kedrick saw them bunch, and when they all were there, he said simply, "All right, let's go!"

They mounted up. Kedrick noted slender wiry Dornie Shaw; the great bulk of Si Fessenden; lean, bitter Poinsett and the square blond Lee Goff; sour-faced Clauson, the oldest of the lot and the lean Texan, Laredo Shad. Moving out, he glanced at them. Whatever else they might be, they were fighting men. Several times Shaw glanced at his guns.

"You ain't wearin' Colts?"

"No, .44 Russians. They are a good gun, one of the most accurate ever built." He indicated the trail ahead with a nod. "You've been out this way before?"

"Yeah, we got quite a ride. We'll noon at a spring I know just over the North Fork. There's some deep canyons to cross, then a big peak. The Indians an' Spanish called it The Orphan. All wild country. Right beyond there we'll begin strikin' a few of 'em." He grinned a little, showing his white even teeth. "They are scattered all over hell's half acre."

"Dornie," Goff asked suddenly, "you figure on ridin' over to the malpais this trip?"

Clauson chuckled. "Sure, he will! He should've give up long ago, but he's sure hard to whip! That girl has set her sights higher'n any West country gun slinger."

"She's shapely, at that!" Goff was openly admiring. "Right shapely, but playin' no fav'rites."

"Maybe they're playin' each other for what they can git," Poinsett said, wryly. "Maybe that's where he gets all the news he's tellin' Keith. He sure seems to know a sight o' what's goin' around."

Dornie Shaw turned in his saddle, and his thin features had sharpened. "Shut up!" he said coldly.

The older man tightened and his eyes blazed back with genuine hate, yet he held his peace. It was educational to see how quickly he quieted down; for Poinsett, a hard, vicious man with no love for anybody or anything, obviously wanted no part of what Shaw could give him.

As the day drew on, Kedrick studied the men,

27

and noticed they all avoided giving offense to Shaw, even the burly Fessenden who had killed twenty men, and was the only one of the group Kedrick had ever seen before. He wondered if Fessenden remembered him and decided he would known before the day was out.

Around the noon camp there was less friendly banter than would occur in a cow camp. These men were surly and touchy. Only Shad seemed able to relax, and everything came easily for him. Clauson seemed to take over the cooking job by tacit consent, and the reason was soon obvious: he was an excellent cook.

As he ate, Tom Kedrick studied his situation with care. He had taken this job in New Orleans, and at the time had needed money badly. Gunter had put up the cash to get him out here. If he did back out, he would have to find a way to repay him. Yet the more he looked over this group, the more he believed that he was in something that he wanted out of—but fast.

He had fought as a soldier of fortune in several wars. War had been his profession, and he had been a skilled fighting man almost from the beginning. His father, a one-time soldier, had a love for tactics, and Tom had grown up with an interest in things military. His education had mostly come from his father and from a newspaper man who lived with them for a winter and helped to teach the boy what he could.

Kedrick had grown up with his interest in tactics, and had entered the army and fought through the War Between the States. The subsequent fighting had given him a practical background to accompany his study and theory. But with all his fighting and killing it had entailed, he had not become callous.

To run a bunch of renegades off the land seemed simple enough and it promised action and excitement. It was a job he could do. Now he was no longer sure it was a job for him. His talk with Dai Reid as well as the attitude of so many of the people in Mustang convinced him that all was not as simple as it had first appeared. Now, before taking a final step, he wanted to survey the situation and see just whom he would be fighting, and where. At the same time, he knew the men who rode with him were going to ask few questions. They would do their killing, collect their money, and ride on.

Of them all, only Shad might think as he did, and Kedrick made a mental note to talk with the Texan before the day was over, find out where he stood and what he knew. He was inclined to agree with Shaw's original judgment, that Shad was one of the best of the lot with a gun. The man's easy way was not only natural to him, he was simply confident. He had that hard confidence that comes only from having measured his own ability and knowing what he could do when the chips were down.

After he finished his coffee he got to his feet and strolled over to the spring, had a drink, then arose and walked to his horse, tightening the cinch he had loosened when they stopped. The air was clear. Despite their lowered voices, he could catch most of what was said.

The first question he missed, but Fessenden's reply he heard. "Don't you fret about him. He's a scrapper from way back, Dornie. I found that out. This here ain't our first meetin'."

Even at this distance and with his horse between

29

him and the circle of men, Kedrick could sense their attention.

"Tried to finagle him out of that Patterson herd up in Injun Territory. He didn't finagle worth a durn."

"What happened?" Goff demanded. "Any shootin'?"

"Some. I was ridin' partners with Chuck Gibbons, the Llano gunman, an' Chuck was always on the prod, sort of. One, two times I figured I might have to shoot it out with him my own self, but wasn't exactly honin' for trouble. We had too good a thing there to bust it up quarrelin'. But Chuck, he was plumb salty, an' when Kedrick faced him an' wouldn't back down or deliver the cattle, Chuck called him."

Fessenden sipped his coffee, while the men waited impatiently. When they could stand the suspense no longer, Goff demanded, "Well, what happened?"

The big man shrugged. "Kedrick's here, ain't he?"

"I mean—what was the story?"

"Gibbons never cleared leather. None of us even seen Kedrick draw, but you could have put a half dollar over the two holes in Chuck's left shirt pocket."

Nobody spoke after that, and Tom Kedrick took his time over the cinch. Then leaving his horse, he walked away further and circled, scouting the terrain thoughtfully.

He was too experienced a man to fail to appreciate the importance of a knowledge of terrain. All this country from Mustang to the Territory line would become a battleground in the near future, and a man's life might depend on what he knew.

He wasted no opportunity to study the country or ask questions.

He had handled tough groups before and he was not disturbed over the problem this one presented. However, in this case he knew the situation was much more serious. In a group the men would be easier to handle than they would separately. These men were all individualists, and were without any group loyalty. In the last analysis, they had faith in only two things: six-gun skill and money. By these they lived and by these they would die.

That Fessenden had talked was pleasing, for it would, at least settle the doubts of some of the others. Knowing him for a gunhand, they would more willingly accept orders from him, not because of fear, but rather because they knew him for one of their own, and not some stranger brought in to command.

When once again they all moved out, taking their time, the heat had increased. Nothing stirred on the wide, shallow face of the desert but a far and lonely buzzard that floated high and alone over a far-off mesa. Tom Kedrick's eyes roamed the country ceaselessly, and yet from time to time his thoughts kept reverting to the girl on the veranda. Connie Duane was a beautiful girl. Although Gunter's niece, she apparently did not approve all he did.

Why was she here? What was her connection with Keith? Kedrick sensed the latter's animosity and he welcomed it. A quiet man, he was slow to anger; but when he was pushed, a deep-seated anger arose within him in a black tide that made him a driving fury. Knowing this rage that lay dormant within him, he rode carefully, talked carefully, and held his temper and his hand.

Dornie Shaw drew up suddenly. "This here is Canyon Largo," he said, waving his hand down the rift before them. "That peak ahead an' on your right is The Orphan. Injuns won't let no white man up there, but they say there's a spring with a good flow of water on top.

"Yonder begins the country that Burwick, Keith and Gunter bought up. They don't have the land solid to the Arizona border, but they've got a big chunk of it. The center of the squatters is a town called Yellow Butte. There's maybe ten, twelve buildin's there, among 'em a store, a stable, corrals, a saloon, an' a bank."

Kedrick nodded thoughtfully. The country before him was high desert country and could under no circumstances be called swamp. In the area where he stood there was little growth: a few patches of curly mesquite grass or black grama, with prickly pear, soapweed, creosote bush and catclaw scattered through it. In some of the washes he saw the deeper green of piñon or juniper.

They pushed on, entered the canyon and emerged from it, heading due west. He rode warily, and once, far off on his left, he glimpsed a horseman. Later, seeing the same rider, nearer than before, he deduced they were under observation and hoped there would be no attack.

"The country where most of the squatters are is right smack dab in the middle o' the range the company is after. The hombre most likely to head 'em is Bob McLennon. He's got him two right-hand men name of Pete Slagle an' Pit Laine. Now, you asked me the other day if they would fight. Them

32

three are shinnery oak. Slagle's an oldish feller, but McLennon's in his forties an' was once a cowtown marshal. Laine, well, he's a tough one to figure, but he packs two guns an' cuts him a wide swath over there. I hear tell he had him some gun trouble up Durango way an' he didn't need no help to handle it."

From behind him Kedrick heard a low voice mutter, "Most as hard to figure as his sister!"

Dornie's mouth tightened, but he gave no other evidence that he had heard. However, the comment served to add a little to Kedrick's information. Obviously, Dornie Shaw had a friend in the enemy's camp, and the information with which he had been supplying Keith must come from that source. Was the girl betraying her own brother and her friends? It could be, but could Shaw come and go among them without danger? Or did he worry himself about it?

There had been no mention of Dai Reid, yet the powerful little Welshman was sure to be a figure wherever he stood. He was definitely a man to be reckoned with.

Suddenly, a rider appeared from an arroyo not thirty yards off and walked her horse toward them. Dornie Shaw swore softly and drew up. As one man, they all stopped.

The girl was small, well made, her skin as brown as that of an Indian, her hair coal black. She had large, beautiful eyes and small hands. Her eyes flashed from Dornie to the others, then clung to Tom Kedrick, measuring him for a long minute. "Who's your friend, Dornie?" she said. "Introduce me."

33

Shaw's eyes were dark and hard as he turned slightly. "Cap'n Kedrick, I want yuh to meet Sue Laine."

"Captain?" She studied him anew. "Were you in the army?"

"Yes," he said quietly. Her pinto was not the horse of the rider who had been observing them; therefore, there was another rider out there somewhere. Who was he?

"You're ridin' quite a ways from home, Sue," Shaw interrupted. "You think that's wise?"

"I can take care of myself, Dornie!" Her reply was cool, and Kedrick saw blood rise under Shaw's skin. "However, I came to warn you, or Captain Kedrick, if he is in charge. It won't be safe to ride any further. McLennon called a meeting this morning and they voted to open fire on any party of surveyors or strange riders they see. From now on, this country is closed. A rider is going to Mustang tonight with the news."

"There she is," Goff said dryly. "They are sure enough askin' for it! What if we ride on, anyway?"

Sue glanced at him. "Then there will be fighting," she said quietly.

"Well," Poinsett said impatiently, "what are we talkin' for? We come here to fight, didn't we? Let's ride on an' see how much battle they got in them."

Tom Kedrick studied the girl thoughtfully. She was pretty, all right, very pretty. She lacked the quiet beauty of Connie Duane, but she did have beauty. "Do they have scouts out?" he asked.

She glanced at him. "Not yet, but they will have." She smiled. "If they had I'd never have dared ride to warn you."

34

"Whose side are you on, Miss Laine?" Kedrick asked.

Dornie's head came around sharply and his eyes blazed. Before he could speak, Sue Laine answered for herself. "That decision I make for myself. My brother does not make it for me, nor any one of them. They are fools! To fight over this desert!" Contemptuously, she waved a hand at it. "There's no more than a bare living on it, anyway! If they lose, maybe we can leave this country!"

She swung her horse abruptly. "Well, you've had your warning. Now I'll go back."

"I'll be ridin' your way," Shaw interposed.

Her eyes swung back to him. "Don't bother!" Then she turned her attention deliberately to Kedrick and measured him again with her cool eyes, a hint of a smile in them now. "If anybody comes, let Captain Kedrick come. They don't know him!"

Somebody in the group chuckled, and Dornie Shaw, his face white as death, swung his horse. His teeth were bared, his right hand poised. "Who laughed?" he said, his voice almost trembling.

"Miss Laine," Kedrick said quietly, "I think Dornie Shaw could make the trip better than I. He knows the country."

Shaw's eyes glittered. "I asked: who laughed?"

Kedrick turned his head. "Forget it, Shaw." His voice was crisp. "There'll be no fighting with other men in this outfit while I'm in command!"

For an instant, Dornie Shaw held his pose. Then his eyes, suddenly opaque as a rattler's, swung toward Kedrick. "You're tellin' *me?*" Incredulity mixed with sarcasm.

Tom Kedrick knew danger when he saw it, but he only nodded. "You, or anybody, Dornie. We have a job to do. You've hired on for that job as much as any man here. If we begin to fight among ourselves we'll get nothing done, and right now we can't afford to lose a good man.

"I scarcely think," he added, "that either Keith or Burwick would like the idea of a killing among their own men."

Shaw's eyes held Kedrick's and for an instant there was no sound. A cicada hummed in the brush, and Sue Laine's horse stamped at a fly. Tom Kedrick knew in that instant that Dornie Shaw hated him. He had an idea that this was the first time Shaw had ever been thwarted in any purpose he held.

Then Shaw's right hand slowly lowered. "Yuh got me on that one, Cap'n," his voice was empty, dry. "I reckon this is too soon to start shootin'— an' old man Burwick is right touchy."

Sue Laine glanced at Kedrick, genuine surprise and not a little respect in her eyes. "I'll be going. Watch yourselves!"

Before her horse could more than start, Kedrick asked, "Miss Laine, which of your outfit rides a long-legged grulla?"

She turned on him, her face pale. "A—a grulla?"

"Yes," he said, "such a rider has been watching us most of the morning, and such a rider is not over a half mile away now. Also," he added, "he has a field glass!"

Fessenden turned with an oath, and Poinsett glared around. Only Shaw spoke. His voice was strained and queer. "A grulla? Here?"

He refused to say more, but Kedrick studied him, puzzled by the remark. It was almost as if Shaw knew a grulla horse, but had not expected it to be seen here. The same might be true of Sue Laine, who

36

was obviously upset by his comment. Long after they rode on, turning back toward the spring on the North Fork, Kedrick puzzled over it. This was an entirely new element that might mean anything or nothing.

There was little talking on the way back. Poinsett was obviously irritated that they had not ridden into a fight, yet he seemed content enough to settle down into another camp.

CHAPTER IV

DORNIE SHAW was silent. Only when Tom Kedrick arose after supper and began to saddle his horse did he look up. Kedrick glanced at him. "Shaw, I'm ridin' to Yellow Butte. I'm going to look that setup over at first hand. I don't want trouble an' I'm not huntin' any, but I want to know what we're tacklin'."

Shaw was standing, staring after him, when he rode off. Kedrick rode swiftly, pushing due west at a good pace to take advantage of the remaining light. He had more than one reason for the ride. He wanted to study the town and the terrain, but also he wanted to see what the people were like. Were they family men? Or were they outlaws? He had seen little thus far that tended to prove the outlaw theory.

The town of Yellow Butte lay huddled at the base of the long oval-shaped mesa from which it took its name. There, on a bit of flat land, the stone and frame buildings of the town had gathered together. Most of them backed against the higher land behind them, and faced toward the arroyo. Only three buildings and the corrals were on the arroyo side, but one thing was obvious. The town had never been planned for defense.

A rifleman or two on top of Yellow Butte could cover any movement in the village; and the town was exposed to fire from both the high ground behind the town and the bed of the arroyo, where there was shelter under its banks. The butte itself was scarcely one hundred and fifty feet higher than the town and looked right down the wide street in front of the buildings.

Obviously, however, some move had been made toward defense—or was in the process of being made—for occasional piles of earth near several of the buildings were plainly from recent digging. He studied them, puzzled over their origin and cause. Finally, he gave up and scouted the area.

Thoughtfully, he glanced at the butte. Had the squatters thought of putting their own riflemen up there? It would seem the obvious thing, yet more than one competent commander, at some time during his career, had forgotten the obvious. It might also be true of these men. He noted that the top of the butte not only commanded the town, but most of the country around, and was the highest point within several miles.

Kedrick turned his palouse down the hill toward the town. He rode in the open, his right hand hanging free at his side. If he was seen, nothing was done to disturb him. What if there were more than one rider?

He swung down before the Butte Saloon and tied his horse at the rail. He knew the animal was weary and in no shape for a long ride.

The street was empty. He stepped up on the walk and pushed through the swinging doors into the bright lights of the interior. A man sitting alone at a table saw him, scowled and started to speak, then thought better of it and went on with his solitaire. Tom Kedrick crossed to the bar. "Rye," he said quietly.

The bartender nodded and poured the drink. It was not until Kedrick dropped his coin on the bar that the bartender looked up. Instantly, his face stiffened. "Who're you?" he demanded. "I never saw you before!"

Kedrick was aware that two men had closed in on him. Both of them were strangers. One was a sharp looking, oldish man, the other an obviously belligerent redhead. "Pour a drink for my friends, too," he said. Then he turned slowly, so they would not mistake his intentions, until his back was to the bar. Carefully, he surveyed the room.

There were a dozen men here, and all eyes were on him. "I'm buying," he said quietly. "Will you gentlemen join me?"

Nobody moved and he shrugged. He turned back to the bar. His drink was gone.

Slowly, he lifted his eyes to the bartender. "I bought a drink," he said quietly.

The man stared back at him, his eyes hard. "Never noticed it," he said.

"I bought a drink, paid my money, and I want what I paid for."

All was still. The men on either side of him leaned on the bar, ignoring him.

"I'm a patient man," he persisted, "I bought a drink, an' I want it—now."

"Mister," the bartender thrust his wide face across the bar, "we don't serve drinks to your kind here. Now get out before we throw you out!"

Kedrick's forearms were resting on the edge of the bar, and what followed was done so swiftly that neither man beside him had a chance to move.

Tom Kedrick's right hand shot out and grabbed the bartender by the shirt collar under his chin, then he turned swiftly, back to the bar, and heaved. The bartender came over the bar as if he were greased and hit the floor with a crash. Instantly, Kedrick spun away from the two men beside him and stood facing the room, gun in hand.

Men had started to their feet, and several had moved toward him. Now they froze where they were. The .44 Russian had appeared as if materialized from thin air.

"Gentlemen," Kedrick said quietly, "I did not come here hunting trouble. I have been hired for a job. I came to see if you were the manner of men you have been represented as being. Evidently your bartender is hard of hearing, or lacking in true hospitality. I ordered a drink.

"You," Kedrick gestured at the man playing solitaire, "look like a man of judgment. You pour my drink and put it on the end of the bar nearest me. Then," his eyes held the room, "pour each of these gentlemen a drink." With his left hand he extracted

40

a gold eagle from his pocket and slapped it on the bar. "That pays."

He took another step back, then coolly, he holstered his gun. Eyes studied him, but nobody moved. The redhead did not like it. He had an urge to show how tough he was and Kedrick could see it building. "You!" Kedrick asked quickly. "Are you married? Children?"

The redhead stared at him, then said, his voice surly, "Yeah, I'm married, an' I got two kids. What's it to you?"

"I told you," Kedrick replied evenly, "I came to see what manner of men you are."

The man who was pouring the drinks looked up. "I'll answer your questions. I'm Pete Slagle."

"I've heard of you."

A slight smile came to Slagle's mouth. "Yeah," he said, "an' I've heard of you."

Nobody moved nor spoke while Slagle calmly poured the drinks. Then he straightened and glanced around the room. "Men," he said, "I reckon there's no use goin' off half cocked an' gettin' somebody killed. Let's give this man a chance to speak his piece. We sure don't have to buy what he wants to sell us if we don't like his argument."

"Thanks, Slagle." Kedrick studied the room. Two of the faces seemed hard, unrelenting. Another was genuinely interested. But at the door in the rear, loitered a man who had shifty eyes and a sour face. He could have been, in disposition at least, a twin brother to the former outlaw, Clauson.

"The land around here," Kedrick said quietly, "is about to be purchased from the Government by the firm that's employed me. The firm of Burwick, Keith and Gunter. In New Orleans, where I was hired, I was told that there were squatters on the land, a bunch of outlaws, renegades and wasters, that they would resist being put off, and would aim to keep the badlands for themselves. My job was to clean them out, to clear the land for the company. I have come here for that purpose."

There was a low murmur from the back of the room. Kedrick took time to toss off his drink, and then calmly began to roll a smoke. To his right, the door opened and two men came in. One of these was as tall as himself with coal black hair turning gray at the temples. His eyes were gray and cold, his face firmly cut. He glanced sharply around the room, then at Kedrick.

"Cap'n Tom Kedrick, Bob," Slagle said quietly, "speakin' his piece. He's just explained that we've been represented as a bunch of renegades."

"That sounds like Burwick," McLennon said. "Get on with it, Kedrick."

"I've little to say but this. Naturally, like any good fighting man, I wanted to look over the terrain. Moreover, since arriving in Mustang certain rumors and hints have reached me that the picture is not one-sided. I have come out here to look you over, to see exactly what sort of people you are, and if you are the outlaws and wasters you have been represented to be. Also, I would like to have a statement from you."

Red's face was ugly. "We got nothin' to say to you, Kedrick," he said harshly, "nothin' at all! Just you come down here with your killers an' see how many get away alive!"

"Wait a minute, Red!" Slagle interrupted. "Let Bob have his say."

"Aw, why bother?" Red said roughly. "The man is

42

scared or he'd never have come huntin' information!"

Kedrick's eyes held Red's thoughtfully, and he
said slowly, "No, Red, I'm not scared. If I decide
the company is right and you are to be run off, that
is exactly what I'll do. If the men I have are not
enough, I'll get more. I'm used to war, Red. I've
been at it all my life, and I know how to win. I'm
not here because I'm scared. I have come simply because I make a pass at being a just man. If you
have a just claim to your places here, and are not
as represented, I'll step out of this.

"Naturally," he added, "I can't speak for the others, but I will tell them of my conclusions."

"Fair enough," McLennon agreed. "All right, I'll
state our case. This land is Government land, like
all of it. The Navajos an' Utes claim some of it, an'
some of us have dickered with them for land. We've
moved in an' settled on this land. Four or five of
us have been here upwards of ten years, most of
us have been here more than three.

"We've barns built, springs cleaned out, some
fences. We've stocked some land, lived through a
few bad summers and worse winters. Some of us
have wives, an' some of us children. We're makin'
homes here. The company is tryin' to gyp us.

"The law says we were to have six months' notice.
That is, it was to be posted six months before the
sale by the Government to the company. This land,
as we understand it, is supposed to be unoccupied.
Well, it ain't. We live on it. Moreover, that notice
was posted five months ago, stuck around in out-
of-the-way places, in print so fine a man can scarcely read it without a magnifyin' glass.

"A month ago one of the boys read it, but it

took him a few days to sort the meanin' out of the legal phrasin', an' then he high-tailed it to me. We ain't got the money to send a man to the Government. So all we can do is fight. That's what we figure on. If the company runs us off, which I don't figure you or nobody can do, they'll buy ever' inch of it with their blood, believe me."

A murmur of approbation went through the room, and Kedrick thoughtfully scanned the faces of the men. Dornie Shaw had judged these men correctly. They would fight. Moreover, with men like McLennon and Slagle to lead them, they would be hard to handle.

Legally, the company seemed to be in the best position; also, the squatters were bucking a stacked deck. From here it would take a man all of two weeks, and possibly three, to get to Washington, let alone cut through all the Government red tape to get to the men who could block the sale—if it could be blocked.

"This here's a speculation on their part," McLennon stated. "There's rumors this here land is goin' into an Injun reservation, an' if it does, that means they'll stick the Government a nice price for the land."

"Or you will," Kedrick replied. "Looks like there's two sides to this question, McLennon. The company has an argument. If the Federal Government does make this a reservation, you'll have to move, anyway."

"We'll face that when it comes," Slagle said. "Right now we're buckin' the company. Our folks aren't speculators. We aren't gunmen, either."

Another man had entered the room, and Kedrick spotted him instantly. It was Burt, the big man he

44

had whipped in the street fight. The man stopped by the wall and surveyed the room.

"None of you?" Kedrick asked gently. "I have heard some stories about Pit Laine."

"Laine's a good man!" Red burst out heatedly. "He'll do to ride any river with!"

Neither McLennon nor Slagle spoke, and the latter shifted his feet uneasily. Evidently, there was a difference of opinion here. He made a note to check on Laine, to find out more about him.

"Well," he said finally, "I reckon I'll study on it a little. In the meantime, let's keep the peace. I'll keep my men off if you will do likewise."

"We aren't huntin' trouble," McLennon said. "As long as there's no shootin' at us, an' as long as the company men stay off our land, there'll be no trouble from us."

"Fact is," Slagle said, "we sent Roberts ridin' in with a message to Burwick to that effect. We ain't huntin' for no trouble."

Kedrick turned toward the door, but the bartender's voice stopped him. "You forgot your change," he said dryly.

Kedrick glanced at him, grinned, then picked the coins up. "Be seein' you," he said and stepped away.

At that instant, the door burst open and a man staggered into the room, his arm about another man, whom he dropped to the floor. "Roberts!" the man said. "He's been murdered!"

All eyes stared at the man on the floor. That he had been shot many times was obvious. He had also been ridden over, for his body was torn and beaten by the hoofs of running horses. Tom Kedrick felt his stomach turn over. Sick with pity and shock, he lifted his eyes.

He looked up into a circle of accusation: Mc-Lennon, shocked and unbelieving; Slagle, horrified; Red and the others crowding closer. "Him!" Red pointed a finger that trembled with his anger. "While he stands an' talks to us, his outfit murders Bob!"

"Git him!" somebody yelled. "Git him! I got a rope!"

Kedrick was standing at the door, and he knew there was no reasoning with these men. Later, they might think and reason that he might have known nothing about the killing of Roberts. Now, they would not listen. As the men yelled, he hurled himself through the swinging doors and jerking loose his reins, hit the saddle of the palouse. The startled horse swung and lined out, not down the street, but between the buildings.

Behind him men shouted and cursed. A shot rang out, and he heard a bullet clip past his head as he swung between the buildings. Then he knew his escape had driven him into a *cul de sac*, for he was now facing—not more than two hundred yards away—the rim around the flat where the town lay. Whether there was a break in that wall he could not guess, but he had an idea both the route up and down along the arroyo would be covered by guards. Swinging his horse, he charged into the darkness toward Yellow Butte itself.

He remembered that coming into town he had noticed a V-shaped opening near its base. Whether there was a cut through the rim there he did not know. It might only be a box canyon, and a worse trap than the one into which he had run on his first break.

He slowed his pace, knowing that silence was the first necessity. If they heard him, he could easily be bottled up. The flat was small, and aside from crossing the arroyo there were but two routes of escape. Both would surely be watched.

The butte towered high above him now, and his horse walked softly forward in the abysmal darkness. Kedrick's safety was a matter of minutes.

The palouse was tired, he knew, for it had been going all day. The riding had been hard and he was a big man. He knew he was in no shape for a hard run against men with fresh horses. The only possible escape lay in some shrewd move that would keep them guessing and give him time. Yet he must be gone before daylight or he was through. By day they would comb this area and surely discover him.

Now the canyon mouth yawned before him. The walls were not high but at least were steep enough to allow no escape on horseback.

The shouts of pursuit had stopped now, but he knew the men were hard at work to find him. By now they would know from the guards on the stream that he was still on the flat, and had not escaped. Those guards might be creatures of his own imagination, but knowing the men with whom he dealt, he felt it was a safe bet that if they had not guarded the openings before his arrival, they certainly would have sent guards out at once.

The canyon was narrow. He rode on, moving with extreme caution, yet when he had gone but a short distance he saw the end of the canyon rising above him, black and somber. His throat tightened and his mouth went dry. The palouse stopped and Tom Kedrick sat silent, feeling the labored breathing of the horse and knowing he faced a stone wall. He was trapped.

Behind him, a light flared briefly, then went out. There was a shout. That had been a struck match—somebody looking for tracks. They had found them. In a few minutes, for they would move cautiously, they would be on him.

There would be no reasoning with them now. They had him. He was trapped!

CHAPTER V

CAPTAIN TOM KEDRICK sat very still, listening. He heard some gravel stir. A stone rattled down the canyon. Every move would count now, and he must take no unnecessary chance. He was cornered, and while he did not want to kill any of these men, he had no intention of being killed.

Carefully, he dismounted. As his boot touched the sand he tested it to make sure no sound would result when his weight settled. Haste now was his greatest danger. There might be nothing he could do, but he was a man of many experiences, and in the past there had always been a way out. Usually there was, if a man took his time and kept his head.

Standing still beside the appaloosa, he studied the situation. His eyes had grown accustomed to the darkness under the bulk of Yellow Butte. He stared around, seeing the faint gray of sand underfoot, the black bulk of boulders and the more ragged stretch of underbrush. Leading his horse, he followed a narrow strip of gray that showed an opening between boulders.

Scarcely wide enough to admit his horse, the opening led back for some twenty feet, then widened. These were low boulders, rising scarcely above his waist, with the brush somewhat higher. The horse seemed to sense the danger, for it, too, walked quietly and almost without sound.

Literally, he was feeling his way in the dark. But he knew that trail of sand must come from somewhere, for water had run here, and that water might spill off the cliff edge, or might come through some opening. Walking steadily, he found himself going deeper into a tangle of boulders, weaving his way along that thin gray trail into he knew not what.

Twice he paused and with his hat, worked back along the path brushing out the tracks. He could not see how good a job he was doing, but the opening was narrow enough to give him a good chance of success. When he had pushed back into the tangle for all of ten minutes, he was brought up sharply by the cliff itself. He had found his way up the slope, through the talus, brush and scattered boulders, to the very face of the rock.

Above him, and apparently out of reach, was a notch in the cliff, and this was probably the source of the sandy trail he had followed. Worried now, he ground-hitched the palouse and moved along the cliff, feeling his way along the face, searching each crack.

49

To his left, he found nothing. Several times he paused to listen, but no sound came from down the canyon. If this was a box canyon, with no exit, the men would probably know it and make no attempt to close in until daylight. In the darkness a man could put up quite a fight in here. Yet, because of their eagerness to avenge the dead man, they might push on.

Speaking softly to the horse, he worked his way along the face to the right, but here the pile of talus fell off sharply and he dipped into a hollow. It was cool and the air felt damp. There might even be a spring there, but he heard no water running.

Despite the coolness he was sweating and he paused, mopping his face and listening. As he stood there he felt a faint breath of wind against his cheek!

He stiffened with surprise, then with a sudden surge of hope, he turned and eagerly explored the rocky face. But could find no source for that breeze. He started on, moving more cautiously. Then the talus began to steepen under his feet, so he worked his way up the cliff alone. He carried his rifle with him.

At the top he could turn and glance back down the canyon at the faint grayness in the distance that indicated the way he had come. Here the canyon turned a bit, ending in a sort of blind alley on an angle from the true direction of the canyon. There, breaking the edge of the cliff above him, was a notch. A steep slide led to the top.

It must have been some vague stirring of wind from up there on the rim that had touched his cheek. He noted that the slide was steeper than a stairway and might start sliding underfoot. Certainly, such a sound would give away his attempt, and it would be the matter of only a few minutes before he would be encircled. As far as that went, the men could even now be patrolling the rim above him.

Turning, his foot went from under him and only a frenzied grasp at some brush kept him from falling into whatever hole he had stumbled upon. Scrambling back to good footing, he dropped a pebble and heard it strike some fifteen or twenty feet down. Working his way along the edge, he reached the foot of the slide and knew what he had come upon.

Water, flooding down that slide during heavy rains, had struck a soft stratum of sand or mud and, striking it with force, had gouged out a deep cut that probably ran back into the canyon itself. There was always a chance that deep within this crack there might be some hiding place, some concealment. Turning abruptly, he returned for his horse.

The slide continued steeply to the bottom of the crevasse scooped from the earth, and when they reached bottom he glanced up. The cut had taken him at least fifteen feet below the regular terrain of the area. Above him he saw a swath of dark sky that stretched about seven feet between the sides of the cut. He led the horse deeper along the narrow bed, and after only a short distance he noted that the top of the cut immediately above him was almost covered by a thick growth of brush growing together from the sides near the top.

It was cool and still down here, and he pushed on until he found a spot where the rush of water had made a turn, and had gouged deeply under the bank, making a sort of cave beneath the overhang. Into this he led his horse, and here he stopped.

A little water stood at the deepest part of the turn, and he allowed the palouse to drink. When the horse had finished, the shallow pool was gone.

Kedrick tried the water in his canteen, then stripped the saddle from the horse and rubbed him down with a handful of coarse grass. Then he tied the horse, and spreading his blanket, rolled up in it. He was philosophical. He had done what he could. If they found him now there was nothing to do but shoot it out where he was.

Surprisingly, he slept, and when he awakened it was the startled breathing of the palouse that warned him. Instantly, he was on his feet, speaking in a whisper to the horse and resting his hand on its shoulder. Day had come, and somewhere above them, yet some distance, there were voices.

The cave in which he stood was dug in sandstone, no more than fifteen feet in depth, and probably eight feet high at the opening. Kedrick moved to the mouth, studied the crevasse down which he had come. It was as he had supposed, a deep-cut water course from the notch in the cliff. Evidently during heavy rains this bed roared full of water, almost to the brim.

At the place where he now stood the brush on either side almost met over the top, and at one point a fallen slab bridged the crack. Glancing back the way he had come, Kedrick saw that much of it was also covered by brush, and there was a chance that he would not be found. A very, very slim chance. He could ask for no more.

He wanted to smoke, but dared not, for the smell of tobacco might warn them of his presence. Several times he heard voices, some of them quite near. He glanced toward the back of the cave and saw the gelding drinking again. Evidently water had seeped through during the night, even though not much. His canteen was over half full, and as yet water was not a problem.

His rifle across his knees, he waited, from time to time staring down the crevasse in the direction he had been going. Where did this water flow? Probably into the arroyo below, near town, and in that case the townspeople would certainly know of it.

Yet as the morning wore on, although he heard occasionally the sound of voices, nobody approached his place of concealment, nor did anyone seem aware of it. Once, he ventured out into the crevasse itself and pulled a few handfuls of grass growing on a slight mound of earth. This he fed to the horse, who ate gratefully. He dug some jerky from his own pack and chewed on it, wishing for a cup of coffee.

Later, he ventured farther down the crevasse, which seemed to dip steeply from where he was. Hearing no voices, he pushed on, coming to a point where the crevasse turned sharply again. The force of the water had hollowed out a huge cave which looked like a bowl standing on edge. Then the water had turned and shot down an even steeper declivity into the black maw of a cavern.

Having come this far he took a chance on leaving his horse alone and walked on down toward the cave. The entrance was high and wide and the cave extended deep into the mountain with several shelves or ledges that seemed to show no signs of water. There was a pool in the bottom, and apparently the water filled a large basin, but lost itself through some cracks in the bottom of the larger hollow.

Although he penetrated no great distance he could find no evidence of another outlet, nor could he feel any motion of air. Yet, as he looked around him, he realized that with some food a man might well hide in this place for weeks, and unless someone went to the foot of the slide and found the opening into the crevasse, this place might never be discovered.

The run-off from the cliff, then, did not go to the arroyo, but ended here, in this deep cavern.

The day wore on slowly. Twice he walked back down to the cavern to smoke, leaving his horse where it was. In a few hours he would try to make his escape. Yet when dusk came, and he worked his way back up the crevasse slide and crawled out on the edge where he could look toward the entrance, he saw two men squatting there beside a fire. They had rifles. They believed him concealed somewhere near and hoped to starve him out.

Kedrick knew that by this time Dornie Shaw must have returned to Mustang with news of his disappearance, and probably, of their murder of the messenger. For he was sure that it had been his own group who had committed the crime. It was scarcely possible that Gunter or Keith would countenance such open violence near town where it could not fail to be seen and reported upon by unfriendly witnesses.

Returning, he studied the slide to the rim. It was barely possible that a horse might scramble up there. It would be no trick for an active man, and the palouse was probably a mountain horse. It was worth a gamble . . . if there was no one on top to

54

greet him. Pulling an armful of grass from near the brush and boulders, he returned to the horse, and watched it gratefully munch the rich green grass.

Connie Duane was disturbed. She had seen the messenger come to her uncle and the others, and had heard their reply. Then, at almost noon the following day, Dornie Shaw and the other men had come in. Tom Kedrick had not returned with them.

Why that should disturb her she could not have said, but the fact remained that it did. Since he had stepped up on the veranda she had thought of little else, remembering the set of his chin, the way he carried his shoulders, and the startled expression when he saw her. There was something about him that was different, not only from the men around her uncle, but from any man she had known before.

Now, when despite herself she had looked forward to his return, he was missing.

John Gunter came out on the veranda, nervously biting the end from a cigar. "What happened?" she asked. "Is something wrong? Where's Captain Kedrick?"

"Wish I knew!" His voice was sharp with anxiety. "He took a ride to look over those squatters an' never came back. I don't trust Shaw, no matter how much Keith does. He's too bloodthirsty. We could get into a lot of trouble here, Connie. That's why I wanted Kedrick. He has judgment, brains."

"Perhaps he decided he wanted no part of it, Uncle. Maybe he decided your squatters were not outlaws or renegades."

Gunter glanced at her sharply. "Who has been talking to you?" he demanded.

55

"No one. It hasn't been necessary. I have walked around town, and I've seen that some of these outlaws, as you call them, have wives and children, that they buy supplies and look like nice, likeable people. I don't like it, Uncle John, and I don't like to think that my money may be financing a part of it."

"Now, now! Don't bother your head over it. You may be sure that Loren and I will do everything we can for your best interests."

"Then drop this whole thing!" she pleaded. "There's no need for it. I've money enough, and I don't want money that comes from depriving others of their homes. They all have a right to live, a chance."

"Of course!" Gunter was impatient. "We've gone over all this before. But I tell you most of those people are trash, and no matter about that, they all will be put off that land, anyway. The Government is going to buy out whoever has control. That will mean us, and that means we'll get a nice, juicy profit."

"From the Government? Your own Government, Uncle?" Connie studied him coolly. "I fail to understand the sort of man who will attempt to defraud his own Government. There are people like that, I suppose, but somehow I never thought I'd find one in my own family."

"Don't be silly, child. You know nothing of business, you aren't practical."

"I suppose not. Only I seem to remember that a lot of worthwhile things don't seem practical at the moment. No," she got to her feet, "I believe I'll withdraw my investment in this deal and buy a small ranch somewhere nearby. I will have no part in it."

"You can't do that!" Gunter exploded impatiently. "Your money is already in, and there's no way of getting it out until this business is closed. Now, why don't you trust me like a good girl? You always have before!"

"Yes, I have, Uncle John, but I never believed you could be dishonest." She studied him frankly. "You aren't very happy about this yourself. You know," she persisted, "those people aren't going to move without a fight. You believed they could be frightened. Well, they can't. I've seen Bob McLennon, and he's not the kind of a man who can be frightened. Even by that choice bunch of murderers Loren has gathered together."

"They aren't that. Not murderers," Gunter protested uneasily, but refused to meet her eyes. "Reckless, yes. And temperamental. Not murderers."

"Not even Dornie Shaw? The nice-looking, boyish one who has killed a dozen men and is so cold blooded and fiendish at times that others are afraid of him? No, Uncle, there is no way you can sidestep this. If you continue, you are going to countenance murder and the killing of innocent people.

"Loren doesn't care. He has always been cold blooded. You've wondered why I wouldn't marry him. That's why. He has the disposition of a tiger. He would kill anything or anyone that stood in his way. Even you, Uncle John."

He started and looked at her uneasily. "Why do you say that?"

"Because it's true. I know our tall and handsome man. He will allow nothing to come between him and what he desires. You've chosen some choice com-

57

panions." She got to her feet. "If you hear anything of Captain Kedrick, let me know, will you?"

Gunter stood still for a long time after she left. He swore bitterly. Connie was like her mother. She always had the faculty for putting her finger on the truth, and certainly, she was right about this. It was beginning to look ugly, but away down deep in his heart, he was upset less over Keith than over Burwick. That strange, fat, and dirty man was a thing of evil, of corruption. There was some foul thing within him, something cold and vicious as a striking snake.

Connie Duane was not the only person who was disturbed over the strange disappearance of Tom Kedrick.

Bob McLennon, unofficial commander of the forces for defense, sat in his rambling ranch house on the edge of Yellow Butte. Pete Slagle, Burt Williams, Dai Reid and Pit Laine were all gathered there. With them was Sue Laine, keeping to the background. Her dark, lovely eyes were stirring from one to the other, her ears were alert for every word.

"Blazes, man!" McLennon said irritably. "Where could he have gone? I'd have sworn he went into that box canyon. There was no other place for him to go—unless he took wings and flew. He had to go in there."

"You looked yourself," Slagle said dryly. "Did you see him? He just ain't there, that's all! He got plumb away."

"He probably did that," Dai Reid commented. "A quick man, that Tom Kedrick. Hand or mind, he's quick." He drew out his pipe and stoked it slowly. "You shouldn't have jumped him," he continued.

"I know the lad, an' he's honest. If he said that was what he come for, it was the truth he told. I'd take my oath he'd no knowledge of the killin'!"

"I'd like to believe that," McLennon agreed. "The man impressed me. We could use an honest man on the other side, one who would temper the wind a bit, or get this thing stopped."

"It won't be that Shaw who stops. He's a murderin' little devil," Slagle said. "He'll kill like a weasel in a chicken pen until there's nought left to kill."

"Kedrick fought me fair," Williams said. "I'll give him that."

"He's a fair man," Dai persisted. "Since a lad I've known him. I'd not be wrong. I'd give fifty acres of my holdin' for the chance to talk to him."

Daylight brought the first attack. It came swiftly, a tight bunch of riders who exploded from the mouth of the arroyo, hit the dusty street of Yellow Butte on a dead run, pistols firing, and then there followed the deep, heavy concussion of dynamite. As suddenly as they had come, they were gone. Two men sprawled in the street.

Peters, the man Shaw had faced down in the streets of Mustang, was one of them. He had taken three .44 slugs through the chest and died before he hit the ground. He had made one fine effort to win back his self-respect. He had seen Dornie Shaw in the van of the charging riders and rushed into the street to get him. He failed to get off a single shot.

The second man down was shot through the thigh and arm. He was a Swede who had just put in his second crop.

The riders had planned their attack well and

had worked near enough 'to the guards at the mouth of the arroyo, and had come at a time when no attack was expected. The one guard awake was knocked down by a charging horse, but miraculously, suffered only bruises. Two bundles of dynamite had been thrown. One had exploded against the door of the general store, smashing it off its hinges and tearing up the porch. The second exploded harmlessly between the buildings.

The first rattle of rifle fire brought Tom Kedrick to an observation point. He had saddled his horse, hoping for a break, and instantly he saw it. The two guards had rushed to the scene of action. Quickly, he led his horse out of the crevasse, rode at a canter to the canyon's mouth. Seeing dust over the town, he swung right and skirting close to the Butte, slipped out into the open—a free man once more.

CHAPTER VI

KEDRICK did not return toward Mustang. He had come this far for a purpose, and he meant to achieve it. Turning west and north, he rode upstream away from Yellow Butte and Mustang. He wanted actually to see some of the homes of which so much had been said. By the way these people lived he could tell the sort they were. It was still morning and all was motionless and warm. Soon he slowed his horse to a walk and studied the terrain.

Certainly, nothing could be farther from swampland. In that, at least, the company had misrepresented. Obviously, they had lied in maintaining that the land was vacant. But if the squatters were a shiftless lot, Kedrick knew he would continue his job. Already he was heartily sick of the whole mess, yet he owed Gunter money, and how to pay it back was a real problem. And then, although the idea lurked almost unthought in the back of his consciousness, there was Connie Duane.

In his fast-moving and active life he had met many women, and a few had interested him, but none so much as this tall girl with the quiet, alert eyes. His desire to get back to Mustang had nothing to do with the company, but only with her. At the same time, Dornie Shaw had acted without his orders, had slain the messenger and attacked the town. For all he knew, Dornie and the others might think him dead.

Turning due north, he rode through the sagebrush and catclaw toward two towering blue mountains. They stood alone this side of the rim that bordered the country to the north. On his left, he saw broken land, and what was evidently a deep arroyo. He swung the appaloosa over and headed it toward the canyon. Suddenly, he reined in.

On the ground before him were the tracks of a trotting horse, and he recognized them. They were the same tracks left by the strange rider on the grulla mustang who had scouted their approach to Yellow Butte. The tracks were fresh.

Riding more slowly, he came to the edge of the canyon and looked down at a long green meadow, fenced and watered by a small stream. At the far side, tucked in a corner, was a stone cottage. It was more attractive and better built than any other he had seen in this section. Ahead of him he saw a trail. Without delay, he rode down it and walked his horse across the meadow toward the house.

It was a pleasant place of sandstone blocks and a thatched roof. Shade trees sheltered the yard, and there were a half-dozen hens pecking about. In the corral there were several horses. His heart jumped as he saw the grulla, saddled and waiting.

He drew up in the dooryard and swung down, trailing his reins. The door opened and a girl came out with a pan of water. She started as she saw him, and he recognized her instantly. It was Sue Laine, the girl of the trail, the girl in whom Dornie was reputed to be interested.

"You!" she gasped as she stared at him. "They told me you were dead!"

He shrugged. "Not dead, just hungry. Could you feed a man?"

She studied him a minute, then nodded. "Come in. Better tie your horse, though. He'll head for that meadow if you don't. And," her voice was dry, "you may need him. This isn't exactly friendly country."

He tied his horse near the grulla and followed her inside. "Isn't it?" he said. "Somehow I gathered you weren't exactly an enemy to the company."

"Don't say that!" she flared. "Don't ever say that!" Her voice lowered. "Not around here, anyway. If my brother ever heard . . ."

So Pit Laine and his sister did not see alike? That was an interesting point. He washed his hands and face, then combed his hair.

Ruefully, he rubbed his chin. "Your brother got a razor? I hate to go unshaven."

She brought a razor without comment. He shaved, then dried his face and hands and walked into the house. It was amazingly neat. On a side table there were several books. Flowered curtains hung at the windows, and several copper dishes were burnished to brightness. He sat down and she brought him food: beef, eggs, and homemade bread with honey.

"Everybody's looking for you," she said. "Where have you been?"

He accepted the statement and ignored the question. "After that messenger was killed, I had to get out of Yellow Butte. I did. What's been happening?"

"Keith served a final ultimatum. We either move, or they run us out. McLennon refused."

"He did right."

She turned on him, her eyes questioning. "You think that? I thought you were their man?"

He looked up from his food and shook his head. "I don't know where I stand, but I don't go for murder, not for running people out of their homes."

"They can't stay, anyway. If this land becomes a reservation they will all be moved off. We will, too. They are foolish to fight."

"At least, the Government will buy their land and pay for their investment. In any event, the company has misrepresented things."

"Does it matter?" She sat down opposite him. "They will win. They have money, influence, and power. The settlers here have nothing." She looked around her bitterly. "Perhaps you think I am going against my own people, but that's not true. These aren't my people. Pit and I don't belong here and we never have, although Pit won't see it. Do you think I want to slave my life away on this desert?"

She leaned toward him. "Look, Captain Kedrick, you're one of them, not just working for them, not just a hired gunman like Dornie Shaw. You can lead the men you have, and I wouldn't be surprised but what you could even handle Keith. You could be a big man in this country, or any country.

"Why be foolish and start thinking like you are? These farmers and ranchers can do nothing for you. They can't even help themselves. The company will win, and if you are one of them, you will have a share in the winning. Don't be foolish, Captain. Stay with them. Do what you have to do."

"There are things more important than money. There's self-respect."

She stared at him, her eyes widening. "You don't really believe that? Try buying supplies with it, sometime. You won't get any place. But that isn't the point. You'll do what you want, but I want a man who will take me out of this desert." She got up quickly and came around the table. "You could do it, Captain. You could become rich, right here."

He smiled at her. "Ambitious, aren't you?"

"Why not? Being a rancher's wife doesn't appeal to me. I want to get away from here, go someplace, be something and enjoy life." She hesitated, studying him. "You could edge Gunter out of it, and Keith—maybe even Burwick. But the first two would be easy, and I know how."

"You do?" He looked up at her. She stood very

close to him, and she was smiling down at him. She was, he had to admit, a lovely girl. And an exciting one. Too exciting for comfort right now, and that was a fact she understood completely. "How?"

She shook her head. "Oh, no! That I'd tell you only if you threw in with me, joined me. But this much I'll tell you—John Gunter is small potatoes. They needed money, and he had that girl's money so they roped him in. Keith is dangerous because he is ambitious and unscrupulous, but the man to reckon with is Burwick. He will be top man when this thing is over, and you can bank on it. He has a way figured, all the time."

"You seem to know a great deal."

"I do. Men like me and men talk. They don't have any idea how much I lead them to say, or how much I remember."

"Why tell me all this?"

"Because you're the man who can do what has to be done. You could whip that bunch into line. All of them would listen to you, even Dornie Shaw —and he's suspicious of you."

"Of me? Why?"

"He saw Dai Reid come from your room. He was watching you."

So that was it? He had suspected that Shaw had something on his mind. But why had Shaw been watching? What was the gunman thinking of? And had he reported that conference to Keith?

Kedrick finished his meal and lighted a cigarette. Ever since their first meeting in the desert this girl had puzzled him. He was inclined to doubt if any girl, reared as she must have been, could be so sincerely disdaining of all loyalty, and so plainly self-seeking. She seemed scarcely more than a child,

65

slim, brown and lovely, with her quick, measuring eyes and her soft lips.

Now, apparently she had selected him as the man who was to take her away from the desert. But how many others held the same idea? However, he had no idea of leaving the desert.

"Your brother around?" he asked.

Her glance was a quick flash of alarm. "You don't want to see him, or talk to him. You'd better get out of here."

"On the contrary, Sue, I'd like to talk to Pit. I've heard about him and I'd like to know him."

"You'd better go," she warned. "He'll be back soon, and some of that Yellow Butte crowd may be with him."

"You mean he's not here? Then whose horse is that out there? That grulla?"

Her face was strange as she shook her head. "You'll think I'm a liar, but I don't know. I never saw the rider."

His eyes searched hers. He could see nothing but sincerity there, sincerity and a little fear. "You mean that horse showed up there, tied like that? And you never saw the rider?"

"That's right. I looked out this morning, shortly after Pit left, and he was tied right there. This isn't the first time! He has been here twice before, when Pit was gone, and some others have seen him, most of them women when their husbands are away. Mrs. Burt Williams said he was tied to her corral for three or four hours one day."

"But surely someone sees the rider come and mount up?"

"Never. He'll be out there like he is now—he's gone!"

Kedrick came to his feet with a start and stared out the door. Sue was right. The mouse-colored horse was gone. His own palouse stood where he had left it, but the grulla had disappeared.

Walking out into the yard, he looked around very carefully. But there was nothing in sight on the plain or the hills. The horse was gone! He looked at her and saw the strained expression on her face. Then he walked out to the appaloosa. Pinned to his saddle was a note. He grabbed it up and glanced at it, then passed it to Sue who had come up beside him.

"Stay away."

Kedrick shrugged. "Your brother do this?"

"Oh, no! I told him about the horse and he knew no more about it than I. Besides, he didn't print that. He couldn't. Pit never learned to either read or write."

Long after he left the malpais arroyo behind, he was puzzling over the strange horse. Somebody was seriously trying either to puzzle or frighten the squatters. Yet it was an action unlike the company. Moreover, it must be somebody who had a lot of time to spend.

Kedrick rode north toward Blue Hill, then swung east, crossing the Old Mormon Trail and skirting the rim.

This was good grazing land. There was an abundance of rough forage here and a good herd of cattle could fatten on this range without trouble. Moreover, the herding problem was solved in part by the rim, which provided a natural drift fence beyond which the cattle could not go.

When he reached Salt Creek he turned down the creek toward the river. Swinging east again and passing near Chimney Rock, he rode southeast until he struck the Hogback Trail. Once over that ridge, he headed due east for Mustang.

Yet as always, his eyes were alive and alert. He loved this land, harsh though it might be at some times. He loved the dim purples and blues, the far-flung mists and morning and night, the gray-green of the sagebrush, and the rust-red of the sandstone. It was a good country, and there was room for all if it were left open for settlement.

His own mind was not yet resolved. The problem of his debt to Gunter weighed heavily upon him, and there were other considerations. He wanted no trouble, and to withdraw now might mean plenty of it. This was especially so if he remained in the country, which he had every reason to do. He would try to talk the company out of withdrawing, but he knew that would fail.

Just where, in all this, did Connie Duane actually stand? Was she involved more deeply than he believed? Or was it only what had been implied, that her uncle had invested her money in the land speculation? If such was the case, it might be difficult or impossible to get out at this stage—even if they would allow it.

Burwick puzzled him. Obviously the controlling power, he gave no evidence of where that power came from aside from some native shrewdness. There might be much more to the man, and evidently there was. That Keith and Gunter deferred to him was obvious.

Purposely, Kedrick had said nothing of his hideaway near Yellow Butte when talking to Sue. That

68

young lady already knew more than was good for her, and that spot might again become useful. It was something to know.

Mustang was asleep when he rode into the town and headed for the stable. He put his horse up and rubbed it thoroughly, gave it a good bait of corn and forked down some hay. Then he made his way quietly to the St. James. As he neared the hotel a tall, lean figure arose from the chair where he himself had been sitting a few days before. The build and the broad hat, the very hang of the guns left no mistake. It was Laredo Shad.

"Cap'n?" The voice was low. "You all right?"

"Yes, and you?"

Shad chuckled. "Don't worry none about Shad! I stay healthy." He motioned to a chair. "You better sit down. I've been hopin' you'd show up."

"What's the talk? Did they think I was dead, or skipped the country?"

"Some o' both, I reckon. Keith was fit to be tied. He wants to see you as soon as you show—no matter when."

"He'll wait. I'm tired."

Shad nodded, then lighted his cigarette, which had gone out. "You know, I ain't right sure about this business."

Kedrick nodded. "I know what you mean. I'm not the man to run folks out of their homes."

"You quittin'?"

"Not yet. I'll talk to 'em first."

"Won't do no good. They are mighty bloodthirsty. It was Poinsett shot that messenger. Dornie put him up to it. Poinsett killed him, an' then four, five of those rannies shot up the body. I don't think Fessenden shot any, an' maybe Goff didn't. You can

69

lay your last peso I didn't shoot none. It was mighty raw, Cap'n, mighty raw!"

"They'll pay for it. Were you on the Yellow Butte raid?"

"Uh huh, but I didn't shoot nobody. I'm no Bible packer, Cap'n, but I do figure a fightin' man shouldn't tackle folks who cain't fight back, an' I ain't the man to be firin' on no women or kids."

"What are they talkin' up now? Any plans you know of?"

Shad hesitated, then shrugged. "Reckon you'd better talk that out with them, Cap'n. I may know somethin' but I ain't tellin', not yet."

The Texan sat silent for a few minutes while both men smoked, and then he waved an impatient hand. "Cap'n, I hired on as a gunhand, an' such I am, but I didn't figure on this sort o' thing. Some of those hombres on the other side o' this shindig look a durned sight more human than some on our own side. I'm gettin' shut o' the whole shebang."

"Uh huh—" surprisingly, Kedrick found resolution coming to him—"I know how you feel, but my own way will be different. I think if I can't talk Gunter an' the rest of them out of that I'll change sides."

Shad nodded. "I've thought of it. I sure have."

Kedrick turned suddenly and found Dornie Shaw standing not twenty feet behind them. Slowly, he got to his feet, and Laredo Shad did likewise. Shaw's eyes avoided Kedrick. "If you figure on leavin' us, Shad, you better figure on killin' me first."

"If I have to," Laredo said quietly, "then I reckon you can die as simple as any other man. Want to try it now?"

"That's enough, Shad!" Kedrick's voice was sharp.

"I've said there would be no more fighting! Not in this outfit!"

Dornie Shaw turned his head slowly and smiled at Kedrick. "Still like to give orders, do you? Maybe that'll be changed."

"Maybe." Tom Kedrick shrugged. "There will be time enough for me to stop giving orders. I'm turning in."

"Keith wants to see you."

"He can wait. I've had a rough time. There's nothing he wants won't wait."

"Shall I tell him that?"

"If you like."

Shaw smiled again. "You must carry a lot o' weight where you come from, Kedrick, but don't forget it ain't here. Keith is a bad man to buck. So's Burwick."

Kedrick shrugged again. "I've bucked worse. But at the moment, I'm bucking nobody. I need sleep, and by the Lord Harry, sleep is what I'll get. Whatever Keith has on his mind can wait until daylight. I'll be up then."

Shaw started to go, then hesitated, unable to restrain his curiosity. "What happened to you? We figured you were dead or taken prisoner when you didn't come back."

For the first time Kedrick began to wonder. Had Shaw wanted the messenger killed for that very reason. Had he deliberately moved that way hoping the enraged settlers would kill Kedrick? It was most likely. "It doesn't matter," he said, passing off the remark casually. "I found a way to keep out of sight."

Shaw turned away, and when he had gone only a few steps, Tom Kedrick spoke up suddenly. "By

71

the way, Dornie. Know anybody who rides a grulla mustang?"

Shaw stopped abruptly, but he did not turn. His whole body had seemed to stiffen. Then he started on. "No," he said gruffly, "I sure don't."

Laredo Shad stared after him. "You know, pardner, you'll either kill that hombre someday or you'll be killed."

"Uh huh," Kedrick said quietly, "I've the same feeling."

CHAPTER VII

KEITH was pacing the floor in the office at the gray stone building when Kedrick walked in. He stopped and turned swiftly. "Shaw tells me you came in after midnight. Why didn't you come to me according to my orders?"

"Frankly, I was tired. Furthermore," Kedrick returned Keith's look, "I'd nothing to report that wouldn't keep."

"You were hired to do a job, and you haven't done it." Keith stood with his hands on his hips. "Where've you been?"

Briefly and clearly, Kedrick explained, omitting only the visit to Laine's and the story of the hideout. "Frankly," he said, "having looked the situation over, I'd say you had small chance of driving those people off. Also, you and Gunter misrepresented things to me and the Government. That land is occupied not by renegades and outlaws, but by good, solid people. You can't get away with running them off."

Keith smiled contemptuously. "Gettin' scared? You were supposed to be a fighting man! As for what we can do or can't do, let me tell you this, Kedrick: we've started to run those people off, and we'll do it! With or without you! Hiring you was Gunter's idea, anyway."

"That's right, it was." Gunter, followed by Burwick, walked into the room, and he glanced swiftly from Kedrick to Keith. "If you're complainin' about his going to look over that country, you can stop. I sent him."

"Did you tell him to come back scared to death? Saying we can't swing it?"

Burwick had been silent, but now he moved to the big chair behind the desk and dropped into it. He sighed heavily and wiped the back of his hand across his mouth, then glanced at Kedrick keenly. "What did you find out?"

"That they are determined to fight. I talked to Bob McLennon and to Slagle. There's no quit in those men. They'll fight at the drop of a hat, and to the last ditch. Right now, at this minute, they are ready for anything. Your raid killed one man, wounded another. The dynamite blasted a door loose and blew a hole in the porch."

Burwick turned swiftly and glared at Keith. "You told me three men dead and a building destroyed! Hereafter you be sure reports to me are accurate."

73

He swung back to Kedrick. "Go on, what happened to you? You got away?"

"I'm here."

Their eyes met and held for a long time. Burwick's stone cold and hard, examining, probing.

"What do you think of the deal?" he asked finally.

"The fight," Kedrick replied carefully, "will raise a stink clear to Washington. Remember the Lincoln County War? We'll have us another general down here, and you know how much profit you'll make out of that place then!"

Burwick nodded his huge head. "Sensible, that's sensible! Have to think our way around that. At least," he glared again at Keith and Gunter, "this man can bring in some sensible ideas and make a coherent report. You two could learn from him."

He looked up at Kedrick. "Anything else?"

"A couple of things. There's a mysterious rider out on those plains. Rides a mouse-colored horse, and he's got those folks more jittery than all your threats."

"Hah?" Burwick was uninterested. He shuffled papers on his desk. "What's this I hear about you quittin'?"

"I won't be a party to murder. These people aren't outlaws, but good, substantial folks. I'd say: buy them out or leave them alone."

"You aren't running this fair!" Keith replied coldly. "We will decide what is to be done."

"Nobody quits," Burwick said quietly, his eyes on Kedrick's, "unless I say so."

Tom Kedrick smiled suddenly. "Then you'd better say so, because I've quit, as of now!"

"Tom!" Gunter protested. "Let's talk this over."

"What of the money you owe the firm?" Keith demanded, unpleasantly. "You can repay that, I suppose?"

"There's no need."

They all turned at the voice. Connie Duane stood in the door. "You have money of mine in this project. When Uncle John got it from me he told me it was a real-estate speculation. His other activities have been honest and practical, so I did not investigate. Now, I have. I shall withdraw my money, and you can pay me less the sum advanced to Captain Kedrick. He may repay me when circumstances permit it."

All in the room were still. Gunter's face was pale, and Keith looked startled, then angry. He started to protest, but he was too slow. Burwick turned on Gunter. "You—" he snorted angrily. "You told me that was your money. You fool! What do you mean, bringing a woman into a deal like this? Well, you brought her in. Now you manage her or I shall."

"Nobody," Connie replied, "is managing me or my affairs from now on. I'll handle them myself!" She turned to Kedrick. "I'm glad, Captain, that you've made this decision. I am sure you'll not be sorry for it."

Kedrick turned to follow her from the room, but Burwick's voice stopped him. "Captain!"

He turned. Keith's eyes were ugly and Gunter's face was haunted by doubt and fear. "Captain Kedrick," Burwick said, "I believe we are all being too hasty. I like your caution in this matter. Your suggestion that cleaning out those people might make trouble and cause talk in Washington is probable. I had considered that, but not knowing McLennon, had considered the chance negligible.

75

"Slagle," he added, "I know. McLennon I do not know. Your suggestion eliminates a frontal attack. We must try some other means. Also," he added, "I believe that your presence has some claim on that of Miss Duane. Consequently, as we can brook no failure now, I have a proposition for you. How would you like to come into the firm? As a silent partner?"

Keith's face flushed angrily, but Gunter looked up, his eyes suddenly hopeful. Burwick continued. "We could give you a fifteen per cent interest, which, believe me, will be adequate. I believe you could keep Miss Duane in line, and with you at the helm we might straighten this whole thing out —without bloodshed."

Kedrick hesitated. The money was a temptation, for he had no desire to be indebted to Connie, yet the money alone would mean nothing. It was that last phrase that gripped his attention and made him incautious. "Without bloodshed," he repeated. "On those terms, I accept. However, let's discuss this matter a bit further."

Keith spun on his heel. "Burwick, this doesn't make sense! You know the only way we'll get those people off is by driving them off. We agreed on that before. Also this man is not reliable. I happen to know that he has friends on the other side and has actually been in communication with them."

"So much the better." Burwick pursed his fat lips and mopped perspiration from his face. "He'll have a contact he can use to make a deal." He chuckled. "Suppose you two run along and let me talk to Captain Kedrick?"

Hours later, Tom Kedrick paused on the street and studied it with care. Burwick had been more than reasonable. Little as he was able to trust him, he thought it possible that Burwick was sincere in his agreement to buy off a few of them, and to try to convince others. Certainly, if the Government moved in they would have to move, anyway. With McLennon and Slagle out of the picture the chances were there would be no fight, for the others lacked leadership. No fighting meant no deaths, and the settlers at least would come out of it with a little money.

He paced the street irritably, avoiding company. Burwick stank of deceit, but the man was a practical man. He realized that a sudden mess of killings preceding the sale of the land would create a furor that might cause them to lose out all around. At least, trouble had been avoided for the time and even Connie was hopeful that something might be done. Tomorrow Kedrick intended returning again to try to make some deal with McLennon and Slagle. A neutral messenger was leaving tonight.

"They won't come to town," Burwick had agreed, "so why not pick some intermediate point? Meet them, say, at Largo Canyon or Chimney Rock? Have your talk there, and I'll come with you. Just you and me, McLennon and Slagle. We can talk there and maybe make peace. Ain't it worth a try?"

It was only that chance for peace that had persuaded him and helped him to persuade Connie. She had listened in silence as he explained the situation. Then she had turned to him frankly. "Captain, you don't trust them, and neither do I. Uncle John has never been this way before, and I believe somehow he has fallen under the domination of those other men. However, I think that if Burwick

77

is willing to talk, we should at least agree. I'll stand by you in this and we'll hope something can come of it that will prevent trouble."

Kedrick was less hopeful than he had let it appear, and now he was studying the situation from every angle. As things stood, it was a stalemate. He was confident that with McLennon and Slagle to lead them, the settlers could manage a stiff defense of their town and their homes. Certainly, they could prevent the survey being completed and prevent any use being made of their lands.

Yet there were fiery elements on both sides, and Keith did not like the turn things had taken. Colonel Loren Keith had from the beginning planned on striking fast and wiping out the opposition. It would be merely another unsolved mystery of the West. Kedrick resolved to keep an eye on the man and be prepared for anything.

He returned to the St. James and to bed, yet he awakened early and was surprised to see Keith mounted and riding out of town at daybreak.

With a bound he was out of bed and dressing. Whatever Keith had in mind, he meant to know. Swiftly, he descended the stairs and went to the livery stable. Mounted, he headed out of town, found Keith's tracks with ease, and followed them. Keith turned off the trail and headed west and slightly north. But after a few miles, Kedrick lost the trail and took a wide swing to try and cut it again. He was unable to. Keith had vanished somewhere in the vicinity of Largo Canyon.

Returning to the hotel he found a message from Bob McLennon. He and Slagle would meet with Burwick and Kedrick at Chimney Rock at three in the afternoon on Wednesday. It was now Monday, and a whole day lay between. Yet during the remainder of Monday he saw nothing of Dornie Shaw, although Laredo Shad appeared a couple of times, then vanished into one of the saloons.

At midnight the door of his room opened slowly and Tom Kedrick, gun in hand, sat up. It was Laredo Shad.

"Somethin's up," he said, dropping on the bed, "an' she looks mighty peculiar. Couple of hours ago Poinsett an' Goff showed up an' said they had quit. No fightin' here, so they were pullin' out for Durango. About a half hour later they mounted up an' took out."

"What's peculiar about that?" Kedrick inquired, building a smoke. "That's in line with Burwick's talk with me."

"Yeah," Shad replied dryly, "but both of them came in here with a good deal of gear. They lost their pack horses somewheres and went out only with what they could carry on the one horse, and durned little o' that."

"What about Fessenden?"

"Ain't seen him."

"Any of the others gone?"

"Clauson is. At least, he ain't around in sight. I ain't seen him since morning."

That left Shaw, who had been around little himself, and Fessenden, if he was still in town. Despite himself, Kedrick was disturbed. But if Burwick was getting rid of his gunfighters it was a good sign, and probably he, Tom Kedrick, was getting too suspicious. Nothing, Shad said, had been said to him about quitting. "In fact," he said dryly, "the Mixus boys pulled in this morning, an' they went right to Burwick."

"Who are they?"

"Killers. Drygulchers, mostly. Bean an' Abe Mixus. They were in that Sandoval affair. Couple of men died awful opportune in that affair, an' come to think of it, Burwick was around. Fact is, that was where I met him."

"Were you in that?"

"Uh uh. I was in town, though, an' had me a run-in with Roy Gangle. Roy was a mighty tough ranny who'd been ramroddin' a big spread down thataway, an' when he got into the war he went bad, plumb bad. We'd had trouble over a steer, an' he braced me. He was a mite slow."

It made no sense—gunmen leaving, but others arriving. Of course, the Mixus boys could have been spoken to before the change of plans. That must be it. He suggested as much to Laredo and the Texan nodded dubiously.

"Maybe. I don't trust that hombre none. Your man Gunter is in over his head. Keith, well, he's all around bad when it comes to that, but neither of them can hold a candle to that Burwick."

Study the situation as he would, Tom Kedrick could see no answer to it, and the fact remained that they were to meet Slagle and McLennon for a peace conference. Out of that anything might come and he had no real cause to distrust Burwick.

The morning was bright and clear with the sun promising a hot day. It was still cool when Kedrick appeared on the street and crossed to the little restaurant where he ate in silence. He was on his second cup of coffee when Connie came in.

Her face brightened with a smile as she saw him,

and she came over to his table. "You know, you're the one bright spot in this place. I'm so tired of that old stone house and seeing that dirty old man around that I can scarcely stand it. I'll be glad when this is all over."

He studied her. "What will you do then?"

"You know, I've not really thought of that. What I want to do is to get a ranch somewhere, a place with trees, grass, and some running water. It doesn't have to be a big place."

"Cattle?"

"A few, but horses are what I want. Horses like that one of yours, I think."

"Good idea. It takes less land for horses, and there's always a market for good stock." He studied the beauty of her mouth, the quietness and humor of her eyes. "Somehow I'm glad to think you're staying. It wouldn't be the same without you. Not now."

She looked at him quickly, her eyes dancing with laughter, but with the hint of a question in their depths. "Why, Tom! That sounds almost like gallantry. Like you were trying to make love to me, like all the cowboys."

"No, Connie," he said quietly, "when I make love to you there won't be any doubt about it. You'll know and I won't be fooling."

"Somehow I think you're right. You wouldn't be fooling."

"Over west of here," he said, "west and south there's a great rim that stretches for miles across the country, and a splendid pine forest atop it. There's trees, water, game, and some of the finest mountain meadows a man ever saw. I know a place over there where I camped once, a good spring, some tall trees, graceful in the wind, and a long sweep of land clear to the rim's edge, and beyond it miles upon miles of rolling, sweeping range and forest."

"It sounds fascinating, like what I've been wanting ever since I came West."

He pushed back his chair. "Maybe when this is over, you'd ride over that way with me? I'd like to show it to you."

She looked up at him. "All right, Tom. We'll look at it together."

He paused, hat in hand, staring out the door. "Together . . ." he mused. Then he glanced down at her. "You know, Connie, that's the most beautiful word in the language—together."

He walked away then, pausing to pay his check and hers, then stepping outside into the warmth of the street. A buckboard had stopped and a man was getting out of it, a man who moved warily and looked half frightened. He glanced around swiftly, then ducked through the door into the store.

CHAPTER VIII

TWO men crossed the street suddenly. One of them was a man Kedrick had never seen before, the other was the sly-looking loafer he had seen hanging around the back door in the saloon at

Yellow Butte. The loafer, a sour-faced man called Singer, was talking. They stopped, and he indicated the buckboard to the man with him. "That's him, Abe," Singer was saying: "He's one of that crowd from across the way. He's brother-in-law to McLennon."

"This is a good place to start," Abe replied shortly, low voiced. "Let's go!"

Tom Kedrick turned on his heel and followed them. As they stepped into the door, he moved forward and caught it before it slammed shut. Neither man seemed to be aware of his presence, for they were intent on the figure at the counter.

"Hello, Sloan," Singer said softly. "Meet Abe Mixus!"

The name must have meant something to Sloan, for he turned, his face gray. He held a baby's bottle, which he was in the act of buying, in his right hand. His eyes, quick and terror stricken, went from one to the other. He was frightened, but puzzled, and he seemed to be fighting for self-control. "You in this squabble, Singer? I figured you to be outside of it."

Singer chuckled. "That's what I aim for folks to think."

Mixus, a lean, stooped man with yellow eyeballs and a thin-cheeked face drew a paper from his pocket. "That's a quit claim deed, Sloan," he said. "You can sign it an' save yourself trouble."

Sloan's face was gray. His eyes went to the deed and seemed to hold there. Then slowly, they lifted. "I can't do that. My wife's havin' a child in the next couple of days. I worked too hard on that place to give it up. I reckon I can't sign."

"I say you better." Mixus' voice was cold, level.

83

The storekeeper had vanished, and the room was empty save for the three, and for Tom Kedrick, standing in the shadows near some hanging jeans and slickers. "I say you better sign because you don't own that prop'ty anyhow. Want to call me a liar?"

Sloan's face was gray and yet resolution seemed to have overcome his immediate fear. He was a brave man, and Kedrick knew that whatever he said now, he would die. Tom Kedrick spoke first.

"No, Abe," he said softly, "I'll call you a liar!"

Mixus stiffened as if struck. He was a killer, and dangerous, but he was a smart, sure-thing killer, and he had believed himself alone but for Singer. Now somebody was behind him. He stood stock still, then started to turn. Singer had fallen back against the wall, his eyes staring to locate Kedrick.

"It's Kedrick!" he said. "The boss gunman!"

Mixus scowled. "What's the matter?" he said irritably. "What yuh buttin' in for?"

"There's to be no more killing, Abe." Kedrick held his ground. "We're havin' a peace conference tomorrow. This killing is over."

"Got my orders," Mixus persisted. "You talk to Burwick."

There was a movement from Sloan, and Mixus whirled on him. "You stand still!" he barked.

"You can go, Sloan," Kedrick said. "Get in your outfit an' head back an' tell McLennon my word is good. You'd better stop thinking about him, Abe. You're in trouble, and I'm the trouble."

Mixus was confused. He knew Kedrick was ramrodding the gunmen for the company, and he was puzzled. Had he been about to do the wrong thing?

84

But no, he had—"You fool!" His confusion burst into fury. "Keith tol' me to git him!"

"Shut up!" Singer yelled. "Dang it! You—"

Abe Mixus was a cold-blooded killer and no heavy-weight mentally. Orders and counter orders had come to him, and worked up to a killing pitch he had been suddenly stopped in the middle of a job and switched off into this back trail where he floundered hopelessly. Now Singer seemed to be turning on him, and he swung toward him, his teeth bared, his face vicious.

"Don't you tell me, you white-livered coyote!" he snarled.

One hand hung over a gun, and Singer, frightened, grabbed for his own gun. Instantly Mixus whipped out his .44 and flame stabbed at Singer. The renegade turned on his heel. His knees slowly buckled and he slid to the floor, his head against a sack of flour, blood welling from his mouth.

Mixus stared down at him, and then slowly, he blinked, then blinked again. Awareness seemed to return to him, and his jittery nerves calmed. He stared down at Singer almost unbelieving.

"Why, I—I—kilt Singer," he said.

"That's right." Kedrick was watching him, knowing now upon what a slender thread of irritation this man's muscles were poised. "What will Keith say to that?"

Cunning came over Abe's horselike face. "Keith? What give you the idee he had anythin' to do with this?" he demanded.

Slowly, attracted by the shooting and made confident by its end, people were gathering in front of the door. The storekeeper had come into the room and stood watching, his face drawn and frightened.

Tom Kedrick took a slow step back as Abe's eyes turned toward the front of the store. Putting the hanging slickers between them, he moved on cat feet to the opening between the counters and slid through into the living quarters and out into the alley behind the store.

Crossing the street below the crowd, he wound up in front of the St. James, pausing there. Laredo Shad materialized beside him. "What happened?" he asked swiftly.

Kedrick explained. "I don't get it," he said. "Keith may be moving on his own. Burwick was to hold off until we had our talk, and I know Keith didn't like that. He spoke right up about it."

"Ain't Singer s'posed to be a settler?" Shad asked. "Won't this serve to get 'em all riled up? Who knew that Singer was with Keith an' the company?"

"You've a point there," Kedrick said thoughtfully. "This may be the very thing that will blow the lid off!"

"Both of them were mighty jumpy. It looked like they had Sloan marked because he was McLennon's relative. I sprung a surprise on them, an' Mixus just couldn't get himself located."

The crowd separated, then gathered in knots along the street to discuss the new event. Shad loitered beside Kedrick, and was standing there when Loren Keith came up. He glanced sharply at Shad, then at Kedrick. "What's happened over there?"

He kept his eyes on Kedrick as he spoke, and Kedrick shrugged. "Shooting, I guess. Not unusual for Mustang from what I hear."

"Mixus was in there," Shad commented. "Wonder if he had a hand in it?"

Keith turned and looked at Laredo, suspicion in his eyes. "Who was shot?" he inquired, his eyes going from one to the other.

"Singer, they tell me," Shad said casually. "I reckon Mixus killed him."

"Mixus? Kill Singer?" Keith shook his head. "That's preposterous!"

"Don't know why," Laredo drawled. "Mixus come heah to fight, didn't he? An' ain't Singer one o' them settlers?"

Colonel Keith hesitated, his sharp, hard features a picture of doubt and uncertainty. Watching him, Kedrick was amused and pleased. The storekeeper had not seen him, and it was doubtful if anyone had but Mixus, the dead man, and the now missing Sloan.

What Abe Mixus would offer as an explanation for shooting Singer, Tom couldn't conceive, but a traitor had died, and the enemy was confounded. Little as it might mean in the long run, it was for the moment a good thing. The only fly in the ointment was the fact that Singer had been a squatter, and that few, if any, knew of his tie-up with Keith and the company.

Watching the crowds in the street, Tom Kedrick began to perceive a new element shaping itself. Public opinion was a force Burwick had not reckoned with, and the faces of the men talking in the streets were hard and bitter.

These were mostly poor men who had made their own way or were engaged in making their way, and they resented the action of the company. Few had known Singer well, and those few had little use for the man. But to them, it wasn't important who was gunned down. To them, it was a fight between a bunch of hard-working men against the company, made up largely of outsiders, seeking to profit from the work of local people. Furthermore, whatever Singer was, he was not a gunman and he was a local man. Abe Mixus was a known killer, a gunman whose gun was for hire.

Tom Kedrick nodded toward the street. "Well, Colonel," he said, "you'd better start thinking about that unless you want to stretch hemp. That bunch is sore."

Keith stared at them nervously, then nodded and hurried away toward headquarters. Shad watched him go and turned toward Kedrick. "You know, we're sort of tied in with the company, an' I don't aim to hang for 'em. Let's light a shuck out of here an' stick in the hills a few days."

"Can't. I've got to make that meeting with Burwick. But you might get out of town, anyway. Scout around and see what you can find of Goff and the others—if they really left the country or not. Meet me at Chimney Rock about sundown tomorrow."

Leaving Shad, Kedrick hurried to his room in the St. James and bundled his gear together. He carried it down to the livery stable and saddled the palouse. When that was done, staying off the main street, he headed for headquarters. It was Connie Duane he wanted to see, and not Burwick or Keith.

There was no sign of any of them. Gunter was not around, and Burwick and Keith seemed to have vanished. Idling in the office, Tom heard a slight movement upstairs. He called out. Feet hurried along the floor above him and then Connie was at the stair head. "Yes?" Recognizing him, she hurried down. "Is something wrong?"

Swiftly he explained, holding nothing back. "Nothing may come of it. But it wouldn't take much to start something. They all know that the company's gunmen are mostly out of town. Burwick, Keith and your uncle must have lit out."

"Uncle John hasn't been around all day. I saw him at breakfast, and then he disappeared."

"I'll look around. Do you have a gun?" He shook his head then. "Don't much think you'll need it. Most of them like you around here, and you've been pretty outspoken. But stay close to your room. The lid's going to blow off."

Before he could reach the door she called to him and he faced her again. "Tom?" He saw the pleading in her eyes. "Be careful, Tom."

Their eyes held for a long moment, and then he nodded. "I will—if I can."

He went out and paused on the steps. Burwick and Keith might get out of the way. But whatever else Gunter might be, he was scarcely the man to leave his niece behind at a time of danger. Puzzled about Gunter's disappearance, Kedrick paused and looked around him. The back street was bare and empty. The white powdery dust lay thickly and had sifted into the foliage of the trees and shrubs.

Kedrick hitched his guns into place and walked slowly around the house. The stable was usually filled with horses. Now it seemed empty. He strode back, his spurs jingling a little, and tiny puffs of dust rising from his boots as he walked.

Once, nearly to the stable, he paused by a water

trough and listened for noise from the town. It was quiet, altogether too quiet. He hesitated, worrying about Connie again, but then went on and into the wide door that gave entrance to the shadowed coolness of the stable.

The stalls were empty, all save one. He walked back, then paused. The chestnut was Gunter's horse, and a saddle lay nearby. Could Gunter be somewhere around town? Kedrick considered that, then dismissed it. He removed his hat and wiped the band with his kerchief, then replaced it. His face was usually thoughtful as he examined every stall.

Nothing.

Puzzled, he stepped out into the bright glare of the sun and heard no sound anywhere. He squinted his eyes around, then saw the ramshackle old building that had done duty for a stable before the present large one was built. He stared at it and then turned in that direction. He had taken scarcely a step when he heard a rattle of hoofs, and swung swiftly around, half crouched, his hands wide.

Then he straightened. Sue Laine slid from her horse and ran to him. "Oh, I've found you, Tom!" she cried, catching him by the arms. "Tom, don't go to that meeting tomorrow. There's going to be trouble!"

"You mean, McLennon's framed something?"

"McLennon?" For an instant she was startled. "Oh, no! Not Mac!" Her expression changed. "Come home with me, Tom. Please do! Let them have this out and get it over with! Come home with me!"

"Why all this sudden worry about me?" He was sincerely puzzled. "We've only met once, and we seem to have different ideas about things."

"Don't stand here and argue! Tom, I mustn't be

seen talking to you—not by either side. Come with me and get away from here until this is all over. I've seen Dornie, and he hates you, Tom. He hates you."

"He does, does he?" He patted her arm. "Run along home now. I've things to do here."

"Oh?" Her eyes hardened a little. "Is it that woman? That Duane girl? I've heard all about her, how beautiful she is, how—how she—what kind of girl is she?"

"She's a lovely person," he said gravely. "You'd like her, Sue."

Sue stiffened. "Would I? I wonder how much you know about women, Tom? Or do you know anything about them? I could never like Connie Duane." She shook his arm. "Come, if you're coming. I just heard this last night, and I can't—I won't see this happen."

"What? What's going to happen?"

She stamped her foot with impatience. "Oh, you fool, you! They plan to kill you, Tom. Now, come on."

"Not now," he said quietly. "I've got to get this fight settled first, then maybe I'll ride your way. Now run along, I've got to look around."

Impatiently, she turned and walked to her horse. In the saddle she glanced back at him. "If you change your mind . . ."

"Not now," he repeated.

"Then be careful. Be careful, Tom."

He watched her go, then happened to glance toward the house. Connie Duane stood in the window, looking down at him. As he looked up, she turned sharply away. He started for the house, then hesitated. There was nothing he could say now, nothing that would have any effect or do any good at all.

He started toward the front of the house again, then stopped. On an impulse he turned and walked swiftly back to the little old building and caught the latch. The door was weathered and gray. It creaked on rusty hinges and opened slowly. Inside there was the musty odor of decay. Kedrick stood there for a minute watching the sunlight filter through the cobwebbed window and fall in a faint square upon the ancient straw that littered the earthen floor. Stepping forward, he peered around the corner of the nearest stall.

John Gunter lay sprawled upon his face, his head pillowed upon one forearm, the back of his shirt covered with a dark, wide stain. Kedrick knelt beside him.

Connie's uncle had been stabbed in the back. Three powerful blows, from the look of the wounds, had been struck downward—evidently while he sat at a desk or table.

He had been dead for several hours.

CHAPTER IX

ALTON BURWICK, for all his weight, sat his saddle easily and rode well. His horse was a blood bay, tall and long limbed. He walked it alongside Tom Kedrick's palouse. From time to time he spurred it to a trot, then eased down. On this morning Burwick wore an ancient gray felt hat, torn at the flat crown, and a soiled neckerchief that concealed the greasy shirt collar.

His shirt bulged over his belt, and he wore one gun, too high on his hip for easy use. His whiskers seemed neither to have grown nor been clipped. They were still a rough stubble of dirty mixed gray. Yet he seemed unusually genial this morning.

"Great country, Kedrick. Country for a man to live in. If this deal goes through you should get yourself a ranch. I aim to."

"Not a bad idea." Kedrick rode with his right hand dangling. "I was talking about that yesterday with Connie Duane."

The smile vanished from Burwick's face. "You talked to her yesterday? What time?"

"Afternoon." Kedrick let his voice become casual, yet he was alert to the change in Burwick's voice. Had Burwick murdered Gunter? Or had it been one of the squatters? With things as they were either would be difficult or impossible to prove. "We had a long talk. She's a fine girl."

Burwick said nothing, but his lips tightened. The red canyon walls lifted high above them. Along here they were nearly five hundred feet above the bottom of Salt Creek. There was but little left to go, and Tom became puzzled by Burwick's increased watchfulness. The man might suspect treachery, but he had said nothing to imply anything of the kind.

Tom's mind reverted to Sue's warning of the previous day—they intended to kill him—but who were "they"? She had not been specific in her warning, except to say that he should not keep this rendezvous today. Kedrick turned the idea over in his mind, wondering if she were deliberately trying to prevent a settlement, or if she knew something and was genuinely worried.

Pit Laine, her gun-slinging brother, was one element in the situation he could not estimate. Laine had not been mentioned in any of the discussions. Although he seemed always just beyond reach, he was definitely in the background as was the mysterious rider of the mouse-colored horse. The whole story of the disappearing seemed fantastic, but Kedrick did not think Sue was inclined to fall for tall stories.

The canyon of Salt Creek widened out and several branch canyons opened into it. They left the creek bed and rode closer together to the towering cliffs, now all of seven hundred feet above the trail. They were heading south, and Burwick, mopping his sweaty face from time to time with a dirty handkerchief, was no longer talking.

Kedrick pushed back his hat and rolled a smoke. He had never seen Burwick so jittery before, and he was puzzled. Deliberately, he had said nothing to any of the company about Gunter, although he had arranged with some of the townspeople to have the body moved. Tom was afraid it might precipitate the very trouble he was trying to end, and bring the fight into open battle. Moreover, he was not at all sure of why Gunter had been killed, or who had done it. That it could be retaliation for Singer's death was an answer to be considered, but it might have been done by either Keith or Burwick.

Suddenly he drew up. A horse coming in alone from the northwest had left recent tracks. Burwick saw them too. "I've seen those tracks before," Tom Kedrick said. "Now whose horse is that?"

"We better step it up," Burwick said, impatiently. "They'll be there before us."

They pushed on into the bright, still morning. The sky overhead was a vast blue dome scattered with fleecy puff-balls of clouds, like balls of cotton on the surface of a lake of pure blue. The red cliffs towered high on their left, and the valley on their right swept away in a vast, gently rolling panorama. Glancing off over this sagebrush-dotted valley, Tom knew that lost in the blue haze, some seven or eight miles away, was Malpais Arroyo and Sue Laine.

Was she there this morning? Or was she riding somewhere else? She was strangely attractive, that slim, dark-haired, dark-eyed girl with her lovely skin, soft despite the desert sun and desert wind. She had come to him, riding all that distance to bring him a warning of danger. Why? Was it simply that she feared for him? Was she in love with him? He dismissed that idea instantly, but continued to wonder. She was, despite her beauty, a hard, calculating little girl, hating the country around, and wanting only to be free of it.

Heat waves danced out over the bottom land, and shadows gathered under the red wall. A dust devil lifted and danced weirdly across the desert, then lost itself among the thick antelope brush and the cat claw. Tom Kedrick mopped his brow and swung his horse farther east. The tall spire of Chimney Rock lifted in the distance, its heavier shouldered companion looming beside and beyond it.

"Look!" Burwick's voice held a note of triumph. "There they come!"

To the south, and still three or four miles off, they could see two riders heading toward Chimney Rock. At this distance they could not be distinguished, but their destination was obvious.

"Now that's fine." Burwick beamed. "They'll be here right on time. Say—" he glanced at his heavy gold watch—"tell you what. You'll be there a shade before them, so what say you wait for them while I have me a look at a ledge up in the canyon?"

Minutes later, Kedrick swung down in the shadow of the rock. There was a small pool of water there. He let the palouse drink and ground-hitched him deeper in the shade, near some grass. Then he walked back and dropping to the ground lit a smoke. He could see the two riders nearing now. One was on a fast-stepping chestnut, the other a dappled gray.

They rode up and swung down. The first man was Pete Slagle, the second a stranger whom Kedrick had not seen before. "Where's McLennon?" he asked.

"He'll be along. He hadn't come in from the ranch, so I came on with Steelman here. He's a good man, an' anything he says goes with all of us. Bob'll be along later, though, if you have to have his word."

"Burwick came. He's over lookin' at a ledge he saw in the canyon over there."

The three men bunched and Steelman studied Kedrick. "Dai Reid tells me you're a good man, trustworthy, he says."

"I aim to be." He drew a last drag on his cigarette and lifted his head to snap it out into the sand.

For an instant, he stood poised, his face blank, then realization hit him. "Look out!" he yelled. "Hit the dirt!"

His voice was drowned in a roar of guns and something smashed him in the body even as he fell. Then something else slugged him atop the head and a vast wave of blackness folded over him, pushing him down, down, down, deeper and deeper into a swirling darkness that closed in tightly around his body, around his throat. And then there was nothing, nothing at all.

Alton Burwick smiled and threw down his cigar. Calmly, he swung into the saddle and rode toward the four men who were riding from behind a low parapet of rocks near the Chimney. As he rode up they were standing, rifles in hand, staring toward the cluster of bloody figures sprawled on the ground in the shade. "Got 'em!" Shaw said. His eyes were hard. "That cleans it up, an' good!"

Fessenden, Clauson and Poinsett stared at the bodies, saying nothing. Lee Goff walked toward them from his vantage point where he had awaited anyone who might have had a chance to escape. He stooped over the three.

Slagle was literally riddled with bullets, his body smashed and bloody. Off to one side lay Steelman, half the top of his head blown off. Captain Kedrick lay sprawled deeper in the shadow, his head bloody, and a dark stain on his body.

"Want I should finish 'em off for sure?" Poinsett asked.

"Finish what off?" Clauson sneered. "Look at 'em —shot to doll rags."

"What about Kedrick?" Fessenden asked. "He dead for sure?"

"Deader'n Columbus," Goff said.

"Hey!" Shaw interrupted. "This ain't McLennon! This here's that Steelman!"

They gathered around. "Sure is!" Burwick swore viciously. "Now we're in trouble. If we don't get McLennon, we're—" His voice trailed away as he looked up at Dornie Shaw. The soft brown eyes were bright and boyish.

"Why, boss," he said softly, dropping his cigarette and rubbing it out with his toe, "I reckon that's where I come in. Leave McLennon to me. I'll hunt him down before sun sets tomorrow."

"Want company?" Poinsett asked.

"Don't need it," Shaw said, "but come along. I hear this Bob McLennon used to be a frontier marshal. I never liked marshals noway."

They drifted to their horses, then moved slowly away. Dornie Shaw, Poinsett and Goff toward the west and Bob McLennon. Alton Burwick, his eyes thoughtful, headed toward the east and Mustang. With him rode the others. Only Fessenden turned nervously and looked back. "We should have made sure they were dead."

"Ride back if you want," Clauson said. "They are dead all right. That Kedrick! I had no use for him. I aimed my shot right for his smart skull."

Afternoon drew on. The sun lowered, and after the sun came coolness. Somewhere a coyote lifted his howl of anguish to the wide white moon and the desert lay still and quiet beneath the sky.

In the deeper shadow of the towering Chimney and its bulkier neighbor there was no movement. A coyote, moving nearer, scented the blood, but with it there was the dreaded man smell. He whined anxiously and drew back, then trotted slowly off, turning only once to look back. The palouse, still ground-hitched, walked along the grass toward the pool, then stopped, nostrils wide at the smell of blood.

Well down behind some rocks and brush, the shooting had only made it lift its head, then return to cropping the thick green grass that grew in the tiny sub-irrigated area around the Chimney. Nothing more moved. The coolness of the night stiffened the dried blood and stiffened the bodies of the men who lay sprawled there.

Ten miles north Laredo Shad, late for his meeting with Kedrick, limped along the trail leading a badly lamed horse. Two hours before, the trail along an arroyo bank had given way and the horse had fallen. The animal's leg was not broken, but was badly injured. Shad swore bitterly and walked on, debating as he had for the past two hours on the advisability of camping for the night. But remembering that Kedrick would be expecting him, he pushed on.

An hour later, still plodding and on blistered feet, he heard horse's hoofs and drew up, slipping his rifle into his hands. Then the rider materialized from the night, and he drew up also. For a long minute no word was said, then Shad spoke. "Name yourself, pardner."

The other rider also held a gun. "Bob McLennon," he said. "Who are you?"

"Laredo Shad. My horse lamed hisself. I'm headed for Chimney Rock. S'pose to meet Kedrick there." He stared at the rider. "Thought you was to be at the meetin'? What happened?"

"I didn't make it. Steelman an' Slagle went. I'm ridin' up here because they never come in."

"What?" Shad's exclamation was sharp. "McLennon, I was right afeared o' that. My bet is there's been dirty work. Nevah trusted that there Burwick, not no way."

McLennon studied the Texan, liking the man, but hesitant. "What's your brand read, Laredo? You a company man?"

Shad shook his head. "Well, now, it's like this. I come in here drawin' warrior pay to do some gun slingin', but I'm a right uppity sort of a gent about some things. This here didn't size up right to me, nor to Kedrick, so we been figurin' on gettin' shut of the company. Kedrick only stayed on hopin' he could make peace. I stayed along with him."

"Get up behind me," McLennon said. "My horse will carry double an' it ain't far."

CHAPTER X

HIS eyes were open a long time before realization came, and he was lying in a clean, orderly place with which he was totally unfamiliar. For a long time he lay there searching his memory for clues to tie all this together. He, himself. He was Captain

Tom Kedrick . . . he had gone west from New Orleans . . . he had taken on a job . . . then he remembered.

There had been a meeting at Chimney Rock and Steelman had come in place of McLennon. He had thrown his cigarette away and had seen those men behind the rocks, seen the sunlight flashing on their rifle barrels. He had yelled and then dropped, but not fast enough. He had been hit in the head, and he had been hit in the body at least once.

How long ago was that? He turned his head and found himself in a square stone room. One side of the room was native rock, and so was part of another side. The rest had been built up from loose stones gathered and shaped to fit. Besides the wide bed on which he lay there was a table and a chair. He turned slightly and the bed creaked. The door opened, and he looked up into the eyes of Connie Duane.

"Connie?" He was surprised. "Where am I? What's happened?"

"You've been unconscious for days," she told him, coming to the bedside. "You have had a bad concussion and you lost a lot of blood before Laredo and Bob McLennon found you."

"What about the others?"

"Both of them were dead. By all rights, you should have been."

"But where are we?"

"It's a cliff dwelling, a lonely one, and very ancient. It is high up in the side of the mountain called Thieving Rock. McLennon knew where it was, and he knew that if word got out that you were alive they would be out to complete the job at once. So McLennon and Shad brought you here."

"Are they still here?"

"Shad is. He hunts and goes to Yellow Butte for supplies, but he has to be very careful because it begins to look like they are beginning to get suspicious."

"McLennon?"

"He's dead, Tom. Dornie Shaw killed him. He went to Mustang to find a doctor for you. He encountered Dornie on the street. Bob was very fast, you know, but Dornie is incredible. He killed Bob before he could get a shot off."

"How did you get here?"

"Bob McLennon and Shad had talked about it, and they knew I was against the company, and also that Uncle John had been killed—so they came to me. I came out here right away. I knew a little about nursing, but not much. Laredo has been wonderful, Tom. He's a true friend."

Kedrick nodded. "Who did the shooting? I thought I saw Poinsett."

"He was one of them. I heard them talking about it but was not sure until later. Poinsett was there, Goff, Fessenden, Clauson and Shaw."

"Anything else happen?"

"Too much. They burned Yellow Butte's saloon and livery stable, and they have driven almost half the people off. Their surveyors are on the land now, checking the survey they made previously. A handful of the squatters have drawn back into the mountains somewhere under Pit Laine and that friend of yours, Dai Reid. They are trying to make a stand there."

"What about Sue?"

She looked at him quickly. "You liked her, didn't you? Well, Sue has taken up with Keith. They are together all the time. He's a big man, now. They've brought in some more gunmen, and the Mixus boys are still here. Right now Alton Burwick and Loren Keith have this country right under their thumbs. In fact, they even called an election."

"An election?"

"Yes, and they counted the ballots themselves. Keith was elected mayor, and Fessenden is sheriff. Burwick stayed out of it, of course, and Dornie Shaw wouldn't take the sheriff's job."

"Looks like they've got everything their own way, doesn't it?" he mused. "So they don't know I'm alive?"

"No. Shad went back there and dug three graves. He buried the other two, and then filled in the third grave and put a marker over it with your name on it."

"Good!" Kedrick was satisfied. He looked up at the girl. "And how do you get out here and back without them becoming curious?"

She flushed slightly. "I haven't been back, Tom. I stayed here with you. There was no chance of going back and forth. I just left everything and came away."

"How long before I can be up?"

"Not long, if you rest. And you've talked enough now."

Kedrick turned over the whole situation in his mind. There could be no more than a few days before the sale of the land would come off, and if there was one thing that mattered it was that the company not be permitted to profit from their crookedness. As he lay there resting, a plan began to form in his mind, and the details supplied themselves one by one.

His guns hung on a nail driven into the wall close to his hand. His duffle, which he had brought away from the St. James, lay in the corner. It was almost dark before he completed his planning, and when Laredo came in he was ready for him.

"Cimarron?" Shad nodded a little later. "Bloomfield would be nearer. How's that?"

"Good." Kedrick agreed. "Make it fast."

"That ain't worryin' me," Laredo said, rolling his tobacco in his jaws. "They've been mighty suspicious lately. Suppose they trail this place down while I'm gone?"

"We'll have to chance that. Here's the message. Hurry it up!"

The sun was bright in the room when Connie came through the door with his breakfast. She turned and her face went white. "Oh, you're up!"

He grinned shakily. "That's right. I've laid abed long enough. How long has it been?"

"Almost two weeks," she told him. "But you mustn't stand up. Sit down and rest."

There was a place by a window where he had a good view of the trail below. At his request Connie brought the Winchester and her own rifle to him. He cleaned them both, oiled them carefully, and placed them beside his window. Then he checked his guns and returned them to their holsters, digging the two Walch Navy pistols from his duffle and checking them also.

He realized that it too was late to do anything now, but it was a wonder he had not thought of Ransome before. No more able legislator existed in Washington than Frederic Ransome, and the two had been brother officers in the War Between the States, as well as friends in France during the Franco-Prussian War when Ransome had been there as an observer. If anybody could block the sale to the company, he could, even on such short notice.

His telegram would be followed by a letter supplying all the details, and with that to go on, Ransome might get something done. He was a popular and able young senator with good connections and an affable manner. Moreover, he was an excellent strategist. It would make all the difference in this situation.

The cliff dwelling was built well back from the face of the cliff, and built evidently with an eye toward concealment as well as defense. They had called this, Connie told him, Thieving Rock, long before the white man appeared, and the Indians who lived here had been notorious thieves. There was a spring, so water was not a worry, and there were supplies enough for immediate purposes.

Two days dragged slowly by, and on the morning of the third Kedrick was resuming his station by the window when he saw a rider coming into the narrow canyon below.

The man was moving slowly and studying the ground as he came. From time to time he paused and searched the area with careful eyes. Kedrick pushed himself up from his chair. Taking the Winchester, he worked his way along the wall to the next room.

"Connie?" he called softly. There was no reply. After a minute, he called a second time. Still there came no answer.

Worried now, he remembered she had said something about going down below to gather some squaw cabbage to add greens to their diet.

Back at the window, he studied the terrain carefully, and then his heart gave a leap. Connie Duane was gathering squaw cabbage from a niche in the canyon wall, not fifty yards from the unknown rider.

Lifting his rifle, Kedrick checked the range. It was all of four hundred yards and a downhill shot. Carefully, he sighted on the rider, then lowered the gun. The stranger was nearer the girl now, and a miss might ricochet and hit her. The canyon wall would throw any bullet he fired back into the canyon itself and it might even ricochet several times in the close confines.

Yet somehow, she had to be warned. If the rider saw her tracks he would find both Connie and the hideout. Suddenly, the ears of the horse came up sharply, and the rider stiffened warily and looked all around. Carefully, Kedrick drew a bead on the man again. He hated to kill an unwarned man, but if necessary he would not hesitate.

Connie was standing straight now and appeared to be listening. Tense in every fiber, Tom Kedrick watched and waited. The two were now within fifty feet of each other, although each was concealed by a corner of rock and some desert growth including a tall cottonwood and some cedars.

Still listening, they both stood rigid. Kedrick touched his lips with the tip of his tongue. His eyes blurred from strain, and he brushed his hand across them.

The rider was swinging to the ground now, and he had drawn a gun. Warily, he stepped away from his ground-hitched horse. Shifting his eyes to Connie, Tom saw the girl wave. Lifting his hand, he waved back. Then he lifted the rifle. She shook a vigorous negation with her arm, and he relaxed, waiting.

Now the man was studying tracks in the sandy bottom of the wash, and as he knelt, his eyes riveted upon the ground, a new element entered the picture. A flicker of movement caught the tail of Kedrick's eye. Turning his head, he saw Laredo Shad riding into the scene. Glancing swiftly at the window, Laredo waved his hand. Then he moved forward and swung to the ground.

From his vantage point Kedrick could hear nothing, but he saw Laredo approach, making heavy going of it in the thick sand. Not a dozen yards from the man, he stopped.

He must have spoken, for the strange rider stiffened as if shot. Slowly he stood erect. As he turned, Tom saw his face full in the sunlight. It was Clauson!

What happened then was too fast for the eye to follow. Somebody must have spoken—who, did not matter. Laredo Shad in a gunman's crouch, flashed his right hand gun. It sprang clear, froze for a long instant, and then just Clauson pulled trigger, Shad fired—but a split second sooner.

Clauson staggered a step back, and Shad fired again. The outlaw went down slowly, and Laredo walked forward and stripped his gun belts from him. Then from his horse he took his saddlebags, rifle and ammunition. Gathering up the dead man and working with Connie's help, together they tied him to the saddle, and then turned the horse loose with a slap on the hip.

Connie Duane's face was white when she came into the room. "You saw that?"

He nodded. "We didn't dare to let him go. If we had we would all have been dead before noon tomorrow. Now," he said with grim satisfaction, "they'll have something to think about."

Shad grinned at him when he came in. "I didn't see that gun he had drawed," he said ruefully. "Had it laying along his leg as he was crouched there. Might've got me."

He dropped the saddlebags. "Mite of grub," he said, "an' some shells. I reckon we can use 'em even though I brought some. The message got off, an' so did the letter. Feller over to the telegraph office was askin' a powerful lot of questions. Seems like they've been hearin' about this scrap."

"Good. The more the better. We can stand it, but the company can't. Hear anything?"

"Uh huh. Somebody from outside the state is startin' a row about Gunter's death. I hear they have you marked for that. That is, the company is sayin' you did it."

Kedrick nodded. "They would try that. Well, in a couple of days I'll be out of here and then we'll see what can be done."

"You take some time," Shad said dubiously. "That passel o' thieves ain't goin' to find us. Although," he said suddenly, "I saw the tracks of that grulla day afore yestiddy, an' not far off."

The grulla again!

Two more days drifted by. With Laredo, Tom Kedrick ventured down the trail and the ladders to the canyon below. They visited their horses concealed in a tiny glade not far away. The palouse nickered and trotted toward him, and Kedrick grinned and scratched his chest. "How's it, boy? Ready to go places?"

"He's achin' for it," Shad said. He lighted a smoke and squinted his eyes at Kedrick. "What you aim to do when you do move?"

"Ride around a little. I aim to see Pit Laine, an' then I'm goin' to start huntin' up every mother's son that was in that dry-gulching. Especially," he added, "Dornie Shaw."

"He's bad," Laredo said quietly. "I nevah seen it, but you ask Connie. Shaw's chain lightnin'. She seen him kill Bob."

"So one of us dies," Kedrick said quietly. "I'd go willing enough to take him with me, an' a few others."

"That's it. He's a killer, but the old bull o' that woods is Alton Burwick, believe me, he is. Keith is just right-hand man for him, an' the fall guy if they need one. Burwick's the pizen mean one."

With Connie they made their start three days later, and rode back trails beyond the Rim to the hideout Laine had established. It was Dai Reid himself who stopped them, and his eyes lighted up when he saw Kedrick.

"Ah, Tom!" His broad face beamed. "Like my own son, you are. We'd heard you were kilt dead."

Pit Laine was standing by the fire, and around him on the ground were a dozen men, most of whom Kedrick recognized. They sat up slowly as the three walked into the open space, and Pit turned. It was the first time Kedrick had seen him, and he was surprised.

He was scarcely taller than his sister, but wide in the shoulders and slim in the hips. When he turned, he faced them squarely, and his eyes were sharp and bitter. This was a killing man, Kedrick de-

109

cided, as dangerous in his own way as that pocket-sized devil, Dornie Shaw.

"I'm Kedrick," he said, "and this is Connie Duane. I believe you know Shad."

"We know all of you." Laine said, watching them, his eyes alert and curious.

Quietly and concisely, Kedrick explained his plan. He ended by saying, "So there it is. I've asked this friend of mine to start an investigation into the whole mess and to block the sale until the truth is clear. Once the sale is halted and that investigation started, they won't be with us long. They could get away with this only if they could keep it covered up, and they had a fair chance of doing that."

"So we wait and let them run off?" Laine demanded.

"No," Tom Kedrick shook his head decidedly. "We ride into Mustang—all of us.

"They have the mayor and the sheriff, but public opinion is largely on our side. Furthermore," he said quietly, "we ride in the minute they get the news the sale is blocked. Once that news is around town they will have no friends. The band-wagon riders will get off, and fast."

"There'll be shootin'," one old-timer opined.

"Some," Kedrick admitted, "but if I have my way there'll be more of hanging. There's killers in that town, the bunch that dry-gulched Steelman and Slagle. The man who killed Bob McLennon is the man I want."

Pit Laine turned. "I want him."

"Sorry, Laine. He killed Bob, an' Bob was only in town to get a doc for me. You may," he added, "get your chance, anyway."

"I'd like a shot at him my own self," Laredo said quietly, "but somethin' else bothers me. Who's this grulla rider? Is he one of you?"

Laine shook his head. "No, he's got us wonderin', too."

"Gets aroun' plenty," the old-timer said, "but nobody ever sees him. I reckon he knows this here country better'n any of us. He must've been aroun' here for a long time."

"What's he want?" Shad wondered. "That don't figure."

Kedrick shrugged. "I'd like to know." He turned to Dai. "It's good to see you. I was afraid you'd had trouble."

"Trouble?" Dai smiled his wide smile. "It's trouble, you say? All my life there's been trouble, and where man is there will be trouble to the end of time, if not of one kind, then another. But I take my trouble as it comes, bye."

He drew deeply on his short-stemmed pipe and glanced at the scar against Kedrick's skull. "Looks like you'd a bit of it yourself. If you'd a less hard skull you'd now be dead."

"I'd not have given a plugged peso for him when I saw him," Laredo said dryly. "The three of them lyin' there, bloody an' shot up. We thought for sure they was all dead. This one, he'd a hole through him, low down an' mean, an' that head of his looked like it had been smashed until we moved him. He was lucky as well as thick skulled."

Morning found Laredo and Kedrick once more in the saddle. Connie Duane had stayed behind with some of the squatters' women. Pushing on toward Mustang, Laredo and Kedrick took their time. They had no desire to be seen or approached by any of the company riders.

"There's nothing much we can do," Kedrick agreed, "but I want to know the lay of the land in town. It's mighty important to be able to figure just what will happen when the news hits the place. Right now, everything is right for them. Alton Burwick and Loren Keith are better off than they ever were.

"Just size it up. They came in here with the land partly held by squatters with a good claim on the land. They managed to get that land surveyed and put in their claim to the best of it, posted the notices and waited them out. If somebody hadn't seen one of those notices and read it, the whole sale might have gone through and nobody the wiser. Somebody did see it, and trouble started. They had two mighty able men to contend with, Slagle and McLennon.

"Well, both of them are dead now. And Steelman, another possible leader is dead, too. So far as they are aware, nobody knows much about the deaths of those men or who caused them. I was the one man they had learned they couldn't depend on, and they think I'm dead. John Gunter brought money into the deal, and he's dead and out of the picture completely.

"A few days more and the sale goes through, the land becomes theirs and there isn't any organized opposition now. Pit Laine and his group will be named as outlaws, and hunted as such, and believe me, once the land sale goes through, Keith will be hunting them with a posse of killers."

"Yeah," Laredo drawled, "they sure got it sewed

up, looks like. But you're forgettin' one thing. You're forgettin' the girl. Connie Duane."

"What about her?"

"Look," Shad said, speaking around his cigarette, "she sloped out of town right after McLennon was killed. They thought she had been talking to you before, and she told 'em off in the office, said she was gettin' her money out of it. All right, so suppose she asks for it, and they can't pay? Suppose," he added, "she begins to talk and tells what she knows, and they must figure it's plenty. She was Gunter's niece, and for all they know he told her more than he did tell her."

"You mean they'll try to get hold of her?"

"What do you think? They'll try to get hold of her, or kill her."

Tom Kedrick's eyes narrowed. "She'll be safe with Laine," he said, but an element of doubt was in his voice. "That's a good crowd."

Shad shrugged. "Maybe. Don't forget that Singer was one of them, but he didn't hesitate to try to kill Sloan, or to point him out for Abe Mixus. He was bought off by the company, so maybe there are others."

At that very moment, in the office of the gray stone building, such a man sat opposite Alton Burwick, while Keith sat in a chair against the wall. The man's name was Hirst. His face was sallow, but determined. "I ain't lyin'!" he said flatly. "I rode all night to git here, slippin' out o' camp on the quiet. She rode in with that gunman, Laredo Shad, and this Kedrick hombre."

"Kedrick! Alive?" Keith sat forward, his face tense.

"Alive as you or me! Had him most of the hair

113

clipped on one side of his head, an' a bad scar there. He sort of favored his side, too. Oh, he'd been shot all right. But he's ridin' now, believe me!"

The renegade had saved the worst until last. He smiled grimly at Burwick. "I can use some money, Mr. Burwick," he said, "an' there's more I could tell you."

Burwick stared at him, his eyes glassy hard, then reached into a drawer and threw two gold eagles on the desk. "All right! What can you tell me?"

"Kedrick sent a message to some hombre in Washington name of Ransome. He's to block the sale of the land until there's a complete investigation."

"What?"

Keith came to his feet, his face ashen. This was beyond his calculations. When the idea of the land grab had first been brought to his attention, it had seemed a very simple, easy way to turn a fast profit. He had excellent connections in Washington through his military career, and with Burwick managing things on the other end and Gunter bringing on the money, it seemed impossible to beat it. He was sure to net a handsome profit, clear his business with Gunter and Burwick, then return East and live quietly on the profits. That it was a crooked deal did not disturb him. But that his friends in the East might learn of it . . .

"Ransome!" His voice was shocked. "Of all people!"

Frederic Ransome had served with him in the war, and their mutual relationshp had been something less than friendly. There had been that episode by the bridge. He flushed at the thought of it, but Ransome knew, and Ransome would use it as a basis for judgment. Kedrick had no way of knowing just how fortunate his choice of Ransome had been.

"That does it!" He got to his feet. "Ransome will bust this wide open and love it."

He was frightened, and Burwick could see it. He sat there, his gross body filling the chair, wearing the same soiled shirt. His eyes followed Keith with irritation and contempt. Was Keith going bad on him now?

"Get back there," Burwick said to Hirst, "and keep me informed of the movements. Watch everything closely now, and don't miss a trick. You will be paid."

When Hirst had gone, Burwick turned to Keith and his fat lips twisted into a smile. "So does it matter if they slow it up a little? Let them have their investigation. It will come too late."

"Too late?" Keith was incredulous. "With such witnesses against us as Kedrick, Shad, Connie and the rest of them?"

"When the time comes," Burwick said quietly, "there will be no witnesses. Believe me, there won't be."

CHAPTER XI

KEITH turned on Burwick, puzzled by the sound of his voice. "What do you mean?" he asked.

Burwick chuckled and rolled his fat lips on his

cigar. There was malice and some contempt in the look he gave Keith. How much better, he thought, if Kedrick had not been so namby-pamby. He was twice the man Keith was, for all the latter's commanding presence.

"Why," he said, "if there's no witnesses, there'll be no case. What can these people in town tell them? What they suspect? Suspicions won't stand in a court of law, nor with that committee. By the time they get here this country will be peaceful and quiet, believe me."

"What do you mean to do?" Keith demanded.

"Do? What is there to do? Get rid of Kedrick, Laredo Shad, and that girl. Then you'll take a posse and clean out that rat's nest back of the Rim. Then who will they talk to? Gunter might have weakened, but he's dead. With the rest of them out of it—"

"Not Connie!" Keith protested. "Not her! For heaven's sake, man!"

Burwick snorted and his lips twisted in an angry sneer as he heaved his bulk from the chair. "Yes, Connie!" he said. "Are you a complete fool, Keith? Or have you gone soft? That girl knows more than all of them. Suppose Gunter talked to her, and he most likely did? She'll know everything—everything, I tell you!"

He paced back across the room, measuring Keith. The fool! He was irritated and angry. The sort of men they made these days, a weak and sniveling crowd. Keith had played out his time. If he finished this job alive—Dornie didn't like Keith. Burwick chuckled suddenly. Dornie! Now there was a man! The way he had killed that Bob McLennon!

"Now get this. Get the boys together. Get Fessenden, Goff, Clauson, Poinsett and the Mixus boys

116

and send them out with Dornie. I want those three killed, you hear me? I want them dead before the week is out—and no bodies, understand?"

Keith touched his dry lips, his eyes haunted. He had bargained for nothing like this. It had all seemed such an easy profit, and only a few poverty-stricken squatters to prevent them from acquiring wealth in a matter of a few months. And everything had started off just as Burwick had suggested, everything had gone so well. Gunter had provided the money, and he had fronted for them in Washington.

Uneasily, now, Keith realized that if trouble was to come it would be he, himself, upon whom the blame would rest. Burwick, somehow, had remained in the background in the transactions back East as much as he, Keith, had been kept in the background here. Yet it would be Keith's guilt if anything went wrong. And with Ransome investigating everything was sure to go wrong.

Of course, he sighed deeply, Burwick was right. There was only one thing to do now. At least Dornie and the others would not hesitate. Suddenly, he remembered something.

"You mentioned Clauson. He's out of it, Burwick. Clauson came in last night, tied to his horse. He had been dead for hours."

"What?" Burwick stopped his pacing and walked up to Keith. "You just remembered?" he held his face inches away from Keith's and glared. "Is anybody backtracking that horse? You blithering idiot; Clauson was dynamite with a gun. If he's dead, shot, it had to be by one of three men, and you know it!"

Burwick's face was dark with passion and he

wheeled and walked the length of the room, swearing in a low, violent voice that shocked Keith with its deep, underlying passion. When he turned again, Burwick's eyes were ugly with fury. "Can't you realize," he demanded hoarsely, "those men are dangerous?

"Every second they are alive means we are in danger! You have seen Dornie in action. Well, believe me, I'd sooner have him after me than Kedrick. I know Kedrick. He's a former Army officer—that's what you're thinking all the time—an officer and a gentleman!

"But he's something more, do you hear? He's more. He's a gentleman—that's true enough. But the man's a fighter, he loves to fight! Under all that calmness and restraint there's a drive and power that Dornie Shaw could never equal. Dornie may be faster, and I think he is, but don't you forget for one instant that Kedrick won't be through until he's down, down and dead!"

Loren Keith was shocked. In his year's association with Burwick he had never seen the man in a passion, and had never heard him speak with such obvious respect, and even—yes, even fear, of any man. What had Alton Burwick seen that he himself had not seen?

He stared at Burwick, puzzled and annoyed, but some of the man's feeling began to transmit itself to him, and he became distinctly uneasy. He bit his lips and watched Burwick pacing angrily.

"It's not only him, but it's Shad. That cool, thin-faced Texan. As for Laine—" Burwick's eyes darkened—"he may be the worst of the lot. He thinks he has a personal stake in this."

"Personal?" Keith looked inquiringly at the older man. "What do you mean?"

Burwick dismissed the question with a gesture. "No matter. They must go, all of them, and right now." He turned and his eyes were cold. "Keith, you fronted for us in Washington. If this thing goes wrong, you're the one who will pay. Now go out there and get busy. You've a little time, and you've the men. Get busy!"

When he had gone, Burwick dropped into his chair and stared blindly before him. Things had gone too far for him to draw back now even if he was so inclined, and he was not. The pity of it was that there had been no better men to be had than Keith and Gunter.

Yet, everything could still go all right, for he would know how to meet any investigating committee, how to soft pedal the trouble, turn it off into a mere cow-country quarrel of no moment and much exaggerated. The absence of any complaining witness would leave the investigators helpless to proceed, and he could make the difficulty seem a mere teapot tempest. Keith was obviously afraid of Ransome. Well, he was not.

Burwick was still sitting there when the little cavalcade of horsemen streamed by, riding out of town on their blood trail. The number had been augmented, he noticed, by four new arrivals, all hard, desperate men. Even without Keith, they might do the job. He heaved himself to his feet and paced across the room, staring out the window. It went badly with him to see Connie Duane die, for he had plans for Connie. Maybe . . . His eyes narrowed.

Out on the desert the wind stirred restlessly, and in the brassy sky above a lone buzzard circled as if aware of the creeping tension that was slowly gripping the country beneath it.

Far to the north, toward Durango, a cattle buyer pulled his team to a halt and studied the sky. There was no hint of storm, yet he had felt uneasy ever since leaving town on his buying trip down to Yellow Butte and Mustang. There had been rumors of trouble down that way. But then, there had been intermittent trouble there for some time, and he was not alarmed. Yet he was somehow uneasy, as though the very air carried a warning.

South of him, and below the Rim, Laredo Shad and Kedrick turned aside from the Mustang trail and headed toward Yellow Butte. It was only a little way out of their line of travel, but both men wanted to see what had happened there. Yet when they approached the town, aside from the blackened ruins of the destroyed buildings, everything seemed peaceful and still. Eight or ten families had moved back into the town and a few had never left. They looked up warily as the two riders drew near, then nodded a greeting.

They knew now that these two were siding with them against the company, but hardship and struggle had wearied them. They watched the two enter the settlement without excitement. The saloon had opened its door in the large, roomy office of the livery stable, and Kedrick and Laredo entered it. A couple of men leaned on the bar, and both turned as they entered, greeted them, and returned to their conversation.

It was growing cool outside and the warmth of the room felt good. Both men stepped to the bar, and Kedrick ordered and paid. Toying with his drink, Shad seemed uneasy. Finally he turned to Tom. "I don't like it," he said, low voiced. "Somehow or other Burwick is goin' to know about Ransome, an' he'll be in a sweat to get Connie out of the way, an' you an' me with her."

Kedrick agreed, for his own mind had been reading signs along the same trail. Now the only way out for the company was to face the committee, if Ransome managed one, with a plausible tale and an accomplished fact, and then let the investigating body make the most of it.

"Burwick's a snake," Shad commented. "He'll never quit wigglin' until the sun goes down for the last time. Not that one. He's in this deep, an' he ain't the man to lose without a fight."

Horses' hoofs sounded on the road outside and when they turned, Pit Laine and Dai Reid were dismounting before the door. They walked in, and Laine looked at Kedrick, then moved on to the bar. Dai appeared worried, but said nothing. After a minute, Laine turned suddenly and went outside. "What's the matter?" Kedrick asked.

"It be worry, bye, and some of it shame, an' all for that sister o' his. Who would think it o' her? To go over to the other side? He's that shy about it, you would scarce believe. When a man looks at him, he thinks it's his sister they are thinkin' on, and how she sold out to that traitor to mankind, that rascal, Keith."

Kedrick shrugged. "Ambition and money do strange things. She has the makings of a woman, too."

Laine opened the door. "Better come out," he said, "we've got trouble."

They crowded outside. Men were hurrying toward the houses, their faces grave. "What is it?" Kedrick asked quickly.

"Burt Williams signaled from the top of the butte. There's riders coming from Mustang, a bunch of them."

As they looked, the small dark figure of a man appeared on the edge of the mesa once more. This time they saw his arm wave: one . . . two . . . three times, and continue until he had waved it six times. When he had completed, he gestured to the southeast. Then he signaled four more times from the southwest.

"Ten riders," Laine spat. "Well, we've got more than that here, but they aren't as salty as that crowd."

Burt Williams, favoring his broken arm, knelt behind a clump of brush on top of Yellow Butte and studied the approaching horsemen through the glass. He knew all in this group by sight but not by favor. One by one he named them off to himself, "Keith, Dornie Shaw, Fessenden an' Goff—Poinsett." He scowled. "No, that ain't Poinsett. That's one o' the Mixus boys. Yep, an' there's the other."

He swung his glass. The four riders spaced well apart, were approaching at a steady pace. None of their faces was familiar. He stared at them awhile, but finally placed only one of them, a bad man from Durango who ran with Port Stockton and the Ketchum outfit. His name was Brokow.

Stirred, he searched the country all around the town for other movement, then turned back to the larger cavalcade of riders. Had he held on a certain high flat a minute longer he would have seen two unmounted men cross it at a stooping run and drop into the wide arroyo northeast of town.

As it was, he had been studying the approaching group for several minutes before he realized that Poinsett was not among them. He was with neither group.

Worried, Williams squinted his eyes against the sun, wondering how he could apprise them of the danger down below, for the absence of Poinsett disturbed him. The man was without doubt one of the most vicious of the company killers. He was a bitter man, made malignant by some dark happening in his past, but filled now with a special sort of venom all his own. Williams would have worried even more had he seen Poinsett at that moment.

The attack had been planned carefully and with all of Keith's skill. He surmised who they would be looking for, and hoped their watcher would overlook the absence of Poinsett. It was Poinsett whom Keith wanted in the right position for he was unquestionably the best of the lot with a rifle.

At that moment, not two hundred yards from town, Poinsett and his companion, Alf Starrett, were hunkered down in a cluster of brush and boulders at one side of the arroyo. Poinsett had his Spencer .56 and was settling into position for his first shot. Starrett, with a fifteen-shot Henry .44 was a half dozen yards away.

Poinsett pulled out a huge silver watch and consulted it. "At half after two, he says. All right, that's when he'll get it." With utmost composure he began to roll a smoke, and Alf Starrett, a hard-faced and wizened little man, noticed that his fingers were steady as he sifted tobacco into the paper.

Bob McLennon had planned the defense of Yellow Butte, if such a defense became necessary. Bob had been something of a hand with a gun, but he definitely had not been a soldier nor even an Indian fighter. Moreover, he had not expected an all out battle for the town. Whatever the reason, he had committed a fatal error. That pile of boulders and brush offered perfect concealment and almost perfect cover while affording complete range of the town, its one street, and the back as well as front of most of the buildings.

Keith had been quick to see the vantage point on his earlier visits to the town. He had carefully planned to have Poinsett and Starrett approach the place some time before the main force moved in. So far, no hitch in the plan had developed.

Poinsett finished his cigarette and took up his rifle, then settled down to a careful watching and checking of the time. He had his orders and they were explicit. He was to fire on the first traget offered after half past two. His first shot must kill.

Shad and Kedrick had returned to the saloon while Pit Laine loitered out front. Dai had gone across the street. Although Laine was out of Poinsett's sight, Dai made a perfect target. The Welshman, however, offered only a fleeting target and Poinsett did not get a chance to fire. In the next instant, however, the opportunity came.

The door of one of the nearest shacks opened and a man came out. He wore a broad-brimmed gray hat, torn at the crown, and a large checked shirt tucked into jeans supported by suspenders. He turned at the door and kissed his wife. Poinsett took careful aim with his .56, choosing as his aiming point the man's left suspender buckle. Taking a good deep breath he held it and squeezed off his shot.

The big bullet struck with a heavy thump. The man took a heavy lurch sidewise, tried to straighten and then went down. His wife ran from the door, screaming. Up the street a door banged and two men ran into the street, staring. Starrett's first shot knocked the rifle from the hand of one, splintering the stock. Poinsett dropped his man, but the fellow began to drag himself, favoring one leg which even from a distance they could see covered with a dark blotch at the knee.

Poinsett was a man without mercy. Coolly and carefully, he squeezed off his second shot. The man stiffened, jerked spasmodically and lay still.

"Missed my man," Alf said, apologetically, "but I ruint his shootin' iron."

Poinsett spat, his eyes cold. "Could happen to anybody," he said philosophically, "but I figured you burnt him anyways."

Within the saloon Kedrick had a glass half to his mouth when the shot boomed. It was followed almost at once by two more, the reports sounding almost as one.

"Blazes!" Shad whirled. "They ain't here yet?"

"They've been here," Kedrick said with quick realization. He swung to the door, glancing up the street. He saw the body of the last man to fall. Leaning out a bit, he glimpsed the other. His lips tightened, for neither man was moving.

"Somebody is up the draw," he explained quickly. "He's got the street covered. Is there a back way?"

Kedrick dove for the door followed by the oth-

125

ers as the bartender indicated the exit. Catching up his shotgun. His pockets were already stuffed with shells. At the door Kedrick halted. Flattening against the wall, he stared up the draw. From here he could see the edge of the bunch of boulders and guessed the fire came from there. "Pinned down," he said. "They are up the draw."

Nobody moved. Kedrick's memory for terrain served him to good purpose now. Recalling the draw he remembered that it was below the level of the town beyond that point. But right there the boulders offered a perfect firing point.

Scattered shots came from down the draw, and nobody spoke. All knew that they could not long withstand the attack.

CHAPTER XII

KEDRICK made up his mind quickly. Defense of the town was now impossible. They would be either wiped out or burned alive if they attempted to remain. "Shad," he said quickly, "get across the street to Dai and Pit. Yell out to the others and get them to fall back, regardless of risk, to the canyon at the foot of Yellow Butte."

He took a step back and glanced at the trap

door to the roof. The bartender saw the intent and shook his head. "You can't do it, boy. They'd git you from down the crick."

"I'm going to chance it. I think they are still too far off. If I can give you folks covering fire you may make it."

"What about you?" Shad demanded.

"I'll make it. Get moving!"

Laredo wheeled and darted to the door, paused an instant and lunged across the street. The bartender hesitated, swore softly, then followed. Kedrick picked up a bottle of the liquor and shoved it into his shirt, then jumped for the edge of the trap door, caught it and pulled himself through into the small attic. Carefully, he studied the situation.

Hot firing came from down stream, and evidently the killers were momentarily stopped there. He hoisted himself through, swung to the ride of the roof, and carefully studied the boulders. Suddenly, he caught a movement, and knew that what he had first believed to be a gray rock was actually a shirt. He took careful aim with his Winchester, then fired.

The gray shirt jumped, and a hand flew up, then fell loose. Instantly a Spencer boomed and a bullet tore a chunk from the ridge near his face and splattered him with splinters. Kedrick moved down roof a bit. Then catching the signal from the window across the street, he deliberately shoved his rifle and head up, fired four fast shots, then two more.

Ducking his head, he reloaded the Winchester. Another bullet smashed the ridgepole. Then a searching fire began, the heavy slugs tearing through the roof about three to four inches below the top.

Kedrick slid down the roof. He hesitated at the edge of the trap door, and seeing a distant figure circling to get behind the men in the wash, he took careful aim and squeezed off his shot. It was all of five hundred yards, and he had only a small bit of darkness at which to aim.

The shot kicked up sand short of the mark by a foot or more as nearly as he could judge. He knew he had missed, but the would-be sniper lost his taste for his circling movement and slid out of sight. Kedrick went down the trap and dropped again into the saloon. Regretfully, he glanced at the stock of whisky, then picked up two more bottles and stuffed them into his pockets.

Hesitating only a second, he lunged across the street for the shelter of the opposite building. The Spencer boomed, and he knew that the hidden marksman had been awaiting this effort. He felt the shock of the bullet, staggered but kept going.

Reaching the opposite side, he felt the coldness of something on his stomach and glanced down. The bottle in his shirt had been broken by the bullet and he smelled to high heaven of good whisky. Picking the glass out of his shirt, he dove for the livery stable and swung into the saddle on the palouse.

The Spencer boomed again and again as he hit the road riding hard, but he made it. The others cheered as he rode pell mell through the canyon mouth and swung to the ground.

"This is no good," Laine said. "They can get behind us on the ridge."

Two men limped in from the draw, having withdrawn from boulder to boulder. Kedrick glanced around. There were fourteen men and women here who were on their feet. One man, the one who had the rifle knocked from his hand, had a shattered arm. The others were slightly wounded. Of them all, he had only seven men able to fight.

Quickly, he gave directions for their retreat. Then with Dai and Shad to hold the canyon mouth and cover them, they started back up the canyon.

Tom Kedrick measured his group thoughtfully. Of Laredo, Dai and Laine, he had no doubts at all. Of these others, he could not be sure. Good men, some of them, and one or two were obviously frightened. Nobody complained, however, and one of the men whose face was pale, took a wounded man's rifle and gave him a shoulder on which to lean. Kedrick led them to the crevasse and down into it.

Amazed, they stared around. "What d'you know?" The bartender spat. "Been here nigh seven year an' never knowed o' this place!"

There were four horses in the group, but they brought them all into the cave. One of the men complained, but Kedrick turned on him. "There's water, but we may be glad to eat horse meat." The man swallowed and stared.

Laine pointed at Kedrick's shirt. "Man, you're bleedin'!"

Kedrick grinned. "That isn't blood, it's whisky. They busted one of the bottles I brought away."

Pit chuckled. "I'd most as soon it was blood," he said, "seems a waste of good likker."

The able men gathered near the escape end of the crevasse, and one of them grinned at Kedrick. "I wondered how you got away so slick. Is there another way out down there?"

He shook his head. "If there is, I don't know it.

I waited and got out through the canyon when it wasn't watched."

Laine's face was serious. "They could hold us in here," he said, anxiously. "We'd be stuck for sure."

Kedrick nodded. "I'm taking an extra canteen and some grub, then I'm going atop the butte to join Burt Williams. I'd like one man with me. From up there we can hold them off, I think."

"I'm your man," Laredo said quietly. "Wait'll I get my gear."

A rifle boomed, and then Dai Reid joined them. "They are comin' up," he said. He glanced at Kedrick. "One man dead in the boulders. I got the look of him by my glass. It was Alf Starrett. Poinsett was the other."

"Starrett was a skunk," Burnett, one of the settlers said, "a low down skunk. He kilt a man up Kansas way, an' a man disappeared from his outfit oncet that occasioned considerable doubt if he didn't git hisself another."

Kedrick turned to Pit Laine. "Looks like your show down here," he said. "Don't open fire until you have to, and don't fire even one shot unless it's needed. We'll be on top."

He led the way out of the crevasse and into the boulders and brush behind it. There was no sign of the attackers, and he surmised they were holed up awaiting the arrival of some supporting fire from the rim back of the canyon.

Tom glanced up at the towering butte. It reared itself all of a hundred and fifty feet above him and most of it was totally without cover. As they waited, a rifle boomed high above them and there was a puff of dust in the canyon mouth. Burt Williams had opened up.

Their first move toward the butte brought fire, and Laredo drew back. "No chance. We'll have to wait until dark. You reckon they'll hit us before then?"

"If they do, they won't get far." Tom Kedrick hunkered well down among the slabs of rock at the foot of the Butte. "We've got us a good firing point right here." He rolled a smoke and lit up. "What are you planning when this is over, Shad? Do you plan to stay here?"

The tall Texan shrugged. "Ain't pondered it much. Reckon that will take care of itself. What you aimin' to do?"

"You know the Mogollons southwest of here? I figured I'd go down there and lay out a ranch for myself." He smoked thoughtfully. "Down in East Texas, before I came west, a fellow arrived there named Ikard. Had some white-faced cattle with him, and you should see 'em! Why, they have more beef on one sorry critter than three longhorns. I figured a man could get himself a few Hereford bulls and start a herd. Might even buy fifty or sixty head for a beginning, and let 'em mix with the longhorns if they like."

"I might go for somethin' like that," Laredo said quietly. "I always wanted to own a ranch. Fact is, I started one once, but had to git shut of it."

He stared down the canyon toward the mouth, his rifle across his knees. He did not look at Kedrick, but he commented casually, "We need luck, Cap'n, plenty of luck."

"Uh huh," Kedrick's face was sober. "I wonder who was on watch up the canyon? Or supposed to be?"

131

"Somebody said his name was Hirst. Sallow-faced hombre."

"We'll have to talk to him. Was he down below?"

"Come to think of it, he wasn't. He must have hid out back there."

"Or sold out. Remember Singer? He wouldn't have been the only one."

Laredo rubbed out the last of his cigarette. "They'll be makin' their play soon. You know, Kedrick, I'd as soon make a break for it, get a couple of horses an' head for Mustang. When we go we might as well take Keith an' that dirty Burwick with us."

Kedrick nodded agreement, but he was thinking of the men below. There were at least four good men aside from Shad, Laine and Dai Reid. That left the numbers not too unevenly balanced. The fighting skill and numbers were slightly on the enemy's side, as they had at least twelve men when the battle opened, and they had lost Starrett. That made the odds eleven to eight unless they had moved up extra men, which was highly probable. Still, they were expecting defense. But an attack might . . .

He studied the situation. Suddenly, a dark shape loomed on the rim of the canyon some hundred and fifty yards off and much higher. The figure lifted his rifle and fired even as both Shad and Kedrick threw down on him with rifles, firing instantly. The man vanished, but whether hit or not they could not tell.

Desultory firing began, and from time to time, they caught glimpses of men advancing from the canyon mouth—never in sight long enough to offer a target, and usually rising from the ground some distance from where they dropped. The afternoon was drawing on, however, and the sun was setting almost in the faces of the attackers, which made their aim uncertain and their movements hesitant. Several times Shad or Kedrick dusted the oncoming party, but they got in no good shots. Twice a rifle boomed from the top of the butte, and once they heard a man cry out as though hit.

"You know, Laredo," Kedrick said suddenly, "it goes against the grain to back up for those coyotes. I'm taking this grub up to Burt. When I come back down, we're going to move down that canyon and see how much stomach they've got for a good scrap."

Shad grinned, his eyes flickering with humor. "That's ace high with me, pardner," he said dryly. "I never was no hand for a hole, an' the women are safe."

"All but one," Kedrick said, "that Missus Taggart who lives in that first house. Her husband got killed and she wouldn't leave."

"Yeah, heard one o' the women folks speak on it. That Taggart never had a chance. Good folks, those two."

Colonel Loren Keith stared gloomily at the towering mass of Yellow Butte. That man atop the butte had them pinned down. Now if they could just get up there. He thought of the men he had commanded in years past, and compared them with these attacking the town. A pack of murderers. How had he got into this, anyway? Why couldn't a man know when he took a turning where it would lead him? It seemed so simple in the beginning to run off a bunch of one-gallused farmers and squatters.

Wealth—he had always wanted wealth, the money to pay his way in the circles where he wanted to travel. But somehow it had always eluded him, and this had seemed a wonderful chance. Bitterly, he stared at the butte and remembered the greasy edge of Burwick's shirt collar, and the malice in his eyes—Burwick who used men as he saw fit, and disposed of them when he was through.

In the beginning it hadn't seemed that way. His own commanding presence, his soldier's stride, his cold clarity of thought, all these had led him to despise Gunter as a mere business man and Burwick as a conniving weakling. But then suddenly Burwick began to show his true self, and all ideas of controlling the whole show left Keith while he stared in shocked horror as the man unmasked. Alton Burwick was no dirty weakling, no mere ugly fat man, but a monster of evil, a man with a brain like a steel trap, stopping at nothing. By his very depth of wickedness he had startled Keith into obedience.

Gunter had wanted to pull out. Only now would Keith admit even to himself the cause of Gunter's death, and he knew he would die as quickly. How many times had he not seen the malevolence in the eyes of Dornie Shaw, and well he knew how close Shaw stood to Burwick. In a sense, they were of a kind.

His feeling of helplessness shocked and horrified Keith. He had always imagined himself a strong man, and had gone his way, domineering and supercilious. Now he saw himself as only a tool in the hands of a man he despised. Yet he was unable to escape. However, deep within him there was the hope that they still would pull their chestnuts from the fire and take the enormous profit the deal promised.

One man stood large in his mind, one man drew all his anger, his hate and bitterness. That man was Tom Kedrick.

From that first day, Kedrick had made him seem a fool. He, Keith, had endeavored to put Kedrick firmly in his place, speaking of his rank and his twelve years of service, and then Kedrick had calmly paraded such an array of military experience that few men could equal, and right before them all. He had not doubted Kedrick, for vaguely now, he remembered some of the stories he had heard of the man. That the story was the truth, and that Kedrick was a friend of Ransome's infuriated him still more.

He stepped into the makeshift saloon and poured a drink, staring at it gloomily. Fessenden came in, Goff with him.

"We goin' to roust them out o' there, Colonel?" Goff asked. "It will be dark, soon."

Keith tossed all his drink. "Yes, right away. Are the rest of them out there?"

"All but Poinsett. He'll be along."

Keith poured another stiff shot and tossed it off as quickly, then followed them into the street of Yellow Butte.

They were all gathered there—all but the Mixus boys, who had followed along toward the canyon, and a couple of the newcomers who had circled

135

to get on the cliff above and beyond the boulders and brush where the squatters had taken refuge.

Poinsett was walking down the road in long strides. He was abreast of the first house when a woman stepped from the door. She was a square-built woman in a faded blue cotton dress and man's shoes, run down at the heel. She held a double-barreled shotgun in her hands. As Poinsett drew abreast of her, she turned on him and fired.

She shot both barrels, at point-blank range, and Poinsett took them right through the middle. Almost torn in two, he hit the ground, gasping once, his blood staining the gray gravel before the shocked eyes of the clustered men.

The woman turned on them, and they saw she was not young. Her square face was red and a few strands of graying hair blew about her face. As she looked at them, her work-roughened hands still clutching the empty shotgun, she motioned at the fallen man in the faded check shirt.

In that moment, the fact that she was fat, growing old, and that her thick legs ended in the grotesque shoes seemed to vanish—and in the blue eyes were no tears. Her chin trembled a little as she said, "He was my man. Taggart never give me much, an' he never had it to give, but in his own way, he loved me. You killed him—all of you. I wish I had more shells."

She turned her back on them. Without another glance, she went into the house and closed the door behind her.

They stood in a grim half circle, each man faced suddenly with the enormity of what they were doing and had done.

Lee Goff was the first to speak. He stood straddle

legged, his thick hard body bulging all his clothes, his blond hair bristling. "Anybody bothers 'that woman," he said, "I'll kill him."

CHAPTER XIII

KEITH led his attack just before dusk and lost two men before the company men withdrew. But the attack had paid off—they had learned of the hole. Dornie Shaw squatted behind the abutment formed by the end wall of the canyon where it opened on the plain near the arroyo. "That makes it easy," he said. "We still got dynamite."

Keith's head came up and he saw Shaw staring at him, his eyes queerly alight. "Or does that go against the grain, Colonel? About ten sticks of dynamite dropped into that crevasse an' Burwick will get what he wants—no bodies."

"If there's a cave back there," Keith objected, "they'd be buried alive!"

Nobody replied. Keith's eyes wandered around to the other men, but their eyes were on the ground. They were shunning responsibility for the act, and only Shaw enjoyed the prospect. Keith suddered. What a fool he had been to get mixed up in this.

A horse's hoof struck stone, and as one man they

looked up. Although they could not see the horse they heard the creak of saddle leather. A spur jingled, and Alton Burwick stood among them.

Loren Keith straightened to his feet and briefly explained the situation. Burwick nodded from time to time, then added, "Use the dynamite. First thing in the morning. That should end it, once and for all."

He drew a cigar from his pocket and bit off the end. "Had a wire. That committee is comin' out, all right. Take them a couple of weeks to get here, an' by that time folks should be over this an' talkin' about somethin' else. I'm figurin' a bonus for you all."

He turned back toward his horse, then stopped and catching Dornie Shaw's eye, jerked his head.

Shaw got up from the fire and followed him, and Keith stared after them, his eyes bitter. Now what? Was he being left out of something else?

Beyond the edge of the firelight and beyond the reach of their ears, Burwick paused and let Shaw come up to him. "Nice work, Dornie," he said. "We make a pair, you an' me."

"Yeah," Dornie nodded. "An' sometimes I think a pair's enough."

"Well," Burwick puffed on his cigar, "I need a good man to side me, an' Gunter's gone—at least."

"That company o' yours," Dornie was almost whispering, "had too many partners, anyway."

"Uh huh," Burwick said quietly, "it still has."

"All right, then." Dornie hitched his guns into a firmer seating on his thighs. "I'll be in to see you in a couple of days at most."

Burwick turned and walked away, and Dornie saw him swing easily to the saddle. He stayed where he was, looking into the darkness and listening to the slow steps of the horse. They had a funny sound—a very funny sound.

When he walked back to the campfire, he was whistling *Green Grow the Lilacs, O*.

The attack came again at daybreak. The company had mustered twenty men, of whom two carried packages of dynamite. This was to be the final blow. The squatters were to be wiped out, once and for all.

Shortly before the arrival of Burwick, Keith and Dornie Shaw, with Fessenden accompanying them, made a careful reconnaissance of the canyon from the rim. What they found pleased them enormously. It was obvious, once the crevasse had been located, that not more than two men could fire from it at once, and the attackers could find plenty of cover from the scattered boulders. In fact, they could get within throwing distance without emerging in the open for more than a few seconds at a time. Much of the squatters' field of fire would be ruined by their proximity to the ground and the rising of the boulders before them.

The attack started well, with all the men moving out. They made twenty yards into the canyon, moving fast. Here, the great slabs fallen from the slope of Yellow Butte crowded them together. And there the attack stopped.

It stopped abruptly, meeting a withering wall of rifle fire—at point-blank range!

Tom Kedrick knew a thing or two about fighting, and he knew full well that the hideout in the crevasse would in the long run become a death-trap. He put himself in Keith's place and decided what that man would do. Then he had his eight men, carrying fourteen rifles, slip like Indians through the darkness to carefully selected firing positions far down the canyon from where Keith would be expecting to find them.

Five of the attackers died in that first burst of fire. As the gunhands broke for cover, two more went down. One dragged himself to the camp of the previous night with a shattered knee cap. He found himself alone.

The wife of Taggart had begun it—the mighty blast of rifle fire completed it.

The company fighters got out of the canyon's mouth, and as one man they moved for their horses. Keith was among them and glad to be going. Dornie Shaw watched him mount up, and swung up alongside him. Behind them, moving carefully as if they were perfectly disciplined troops, the defenders of the canyon moved down, firing as they came. A horse dropped, and a man crawled into the rocks, then jumped up and ran. Dai Reid swung wide of the group and started after him.

Another went down before they got away, and Kedrick turned to his group. "Get your horses, men. The women will be all right. This is a job that needs finishing now."

A quarter of a mile away, Brokow spotted a horse, standing alone, and started for it. As he arose from the rocks, a voice called out from behind. "A minute!"

Brokow turned. He saw only one man approaching him, the Welshman, Dai Reid. He stared at the man's Spencer, remembering his own gun was empty. He backed up slowly, his eyes haunted.

"My rifle's empty," he said, "an' I've lost my Colt."

"Drop the rifle then," Dai said quietly. "This I've been wanting, for guns be not my way."

Brokow did not understand, but he dropped his rifle. He was a big man, hulking and considered powerful. He watched in amazement as Reid placed his Spencer carefully on the ground, and then his gun belt. With bowlegged strides, the shorter man started for Brokow.

The outlaw stared, then started forward to meet Dai. As they drew near, he swung. His rocklike first smashed Dai Reid flush on the chin. But Reid only blinked, then lunged. Twice more Brokow swung, blows filled with smashing panic born of the lack of effect of that first punch. Dai was unable to avoid the blows, and both connected solidly. But then Dai's huge, big-knuckled hand grasped Brokow's arm and jerked him near.

The hand slipped to the back of his head and jerked Brokow's face down to meet the rising of the Welshman's head. Stars burst before Brokow's eyes, and he felt the bone go in his nose. He swung wildly, and then those big hands gripped his throat and squeezed till Brokow was dead. Then Dai Reid dropped the outlaw to the sand. Turning, he walked away. He did not notice the horse that stood waiting. It was a grulla.

In the headlong flight that followed the debacle in the canyon's mouth, only Lee Goff had purpose. The hard-bitten Montana gunman had stared reality in the face when Taggart's wife turned on him. It was only coincidence that she so resembled his own mother, long since dead of overwork in rearing seven boys and five girls on a bleak Montana ranch.

He headed directly for Yellow Butte and the Tag-

141

gart home. He did not dismount, but stopped by the door and knocked gently. It opened and he faced Mrs. Taggart, her eyes red from weeping. "Ma'am," he said, "I guess I ain't much account, but this here's been too much. I'm driftin'. Will you take this here—as a favor to me?"

He shoved a thick roll of bills at her, his face flushing deep red. For an instant, she hesitated, and then she accepted the money with dignity. "Thanks, son. You're a good boy."

Goff put spurs to his horse and swung it around. The bald-faced sorrel disappeared into the darkness of the night. Lee Goff had had his belly full. He was heading for Colorado, or Utah—anywhere . . . but away.

Elsewhere, Tom Kedrick was riding to Mustang. With him were Laredo Shad, Pit Laine, Dai Reid, Burt Williams, and the others. They made a tight, grim-faced little cavalcade, and they rode with their rifles across their saddle forks.

Due west of them, however, another little drama was taking place. The riders they followed did not include all the men who had abandoned the fight in the canyon. Two of them, Dornie Shaw and Colonel Loren Keith, had headed due west on their own. Both of them had their own thoughts and their own ideas of what to do. Among other things, Keith had decided that he had had enough. Whether the others knew it or not, they were through, and he was getting out of the country.

There was some money back there in Mustang, and once he had that, he was going to mount up and head for California Then let Ransome investigate. After a few years he would return to the East. If the subject ever came up, he would swear he had nothing to do with it, that he only represented the company legally in the first steps of the venture.

What Dornie Shaw was thinking nobody ever guessed. At this moment, however, he had no thought at all in his mind. For his mind was not overly given to thought. He liked a few things, although he rarely drank, and seemed never to eat much. He liked a good horse and a woman with about an equal degree of affection, and he had liked Sue Laine a good bit. However, the woman who really fascinated him was Connie Duane, and she seemed unaware that he was alive.

Most of all he liked a gun. When cornered or braced into a fight, he killed as naturally and simply as most men eat. He was a creature of destruction, pure and simple. Never in his life had he been faced with a man who made him doubt his skill, and never had he fought with anything but guns —and he vowed he never would.

The two rode rapidly and both were mounted well. By the time Kedrick was leaving Yellow Butte with his men and lining out for town, Shaw and Keith reached the bank of Salt Creek Wash. Here Keith swung down to tighten his saddle cinch while his horse was drinking. After a moment, Dornie got down, too.

Absently Keith asked, "Well, Dornie, this breaks it, so where do you think you'll go now?"

"Why, Colonel," Shaw said softly, in his gentle boy's voice. "I don't know exactly where I'm goin, but this here's as far as you go."

It took a minute for the remark to sink in, and then Keith turned, his puzzled expression stiffening into black horror, then fear. Dornie Shaw stood

143

negligently watching him, his lips smiling a little, his eyes opaque and empty.

The realization left Loren Keith icy cold. Dornie Shaw was going to kill him.

He had been an utter fool ever to allow this to happen. Why had he left the others and come off with Shaw? Why hadn't he killed him long since, from behind if need be, for the man was like a mad dog. He was insane, completely insane.

"What's on your mind, Shaw?" Without realizing it he spoke as he might to a subordinate. Shaw was not conscious of the tone. He was looking at Keith's belt line. The Colonel, he reflected, had been taking on a little weight lately.

"Why, just what I say. You've come as far as your trail takes you, Colonel. I can't say I'm sorry."

"Burwick won't like this. We're two of the men on whom he relies."

"Uh huh, that's the way it was. It ain't now. Back yonder," he jerked his head toward the Butte, "he sort of implied he'd got hisself one too many partners." He shoved his hat back a little. "You want to try for your gun? It won't help you none, but you can try."

Keith was frightened. Every muscle within him seemed to have tightened until he could not move, yet he knew he was going to. But at the last, he had something to say, and it came from some deep inner conviction. "Kedrick will kill you, Dornie. He's going to win. He'll beat Burwick, too."

Suddenly, he remembered something: it had been only a fleeting expression on Dornie Shaw's face, but something. "Dornie!" he shot the word out with the force of desperation. "There behind you! The grulla!"

144

Shaw whirled, his face white, an almost animal-like fury on it. As he turned, Keith, gasping hoarsely and triumphantly, grabbed for his gun. He got it, and the gun swung up. But he had never coped with a fighter like Shaw. In the flashing instant that he whirled and found nothing behind him, Dornie hurled himself backward. The shot split wide the air where he had stood an instant before, and then Dornie himself fired from the ground. He fired once, then a second time.

Keith caught the bullet through the midsection, right where that extra weight had been gathering, and took the second one in the same place.

He fell, half in the trickle of water that comprised Salt Creek. Feeding shells into his gun, Dornie Shaw stared down at the glazing eyes. "How did you know?" he asked sullenly. "How did you know?"

CHAPTER XIV

FESSENDEN rode well forward in the saddle, his great bulk carried easily with the movement of the horse. His wide face was somber with thought and distaste. Like the others, the wife of Taggart had affected him as nothing else could have. He was a hard man who had done more than his share of killing. But he had killed men ruthlessly, thoughtlessly, killed men in mortal combat where he himself might die as easily.

Several times before he had hired his gun, but each time in cattle or sheep wars or struggles with equals, men as gun-wise as he himself. Never before had he actually joined in a move to rob men of their homes. Without conscience in the usual sense, he had it in this case. For the men who moved West, regardless of their brand, were largely men in search of homes. Before, he had thought little of their fight. Several times he had helped to drive nesters from cattle range, and to him that was just and logical. Cows needed grass and people lived on beef, and most of the range country wasn't suited to farming, anyway.

But now there was a difference, he realized, thinking of it for the first time. Now men were not being driven off for cattle, but only for profit. To many, the line was a fine one to draw; to Fessenden and his like, once the matter was seen in its true light, that line became a gap, an enormous one.

Actually, he rode in a state of shock. The victory Keith had wanted seemed so near. The taking of the few left in the canyon had seemed simple. His qualms against the use of dynamite he had shrugged off, if uncomfortably. He had gone into the canyon with the others to get the thing over with, to get his money and get out. And then, long before they expected it, came that smashing thunderous volley. It had been made more crashing by the close canyon walls, more destructive by the way the attackers were channeled by the boulders.

Shock started the panic, and distaste for the

whole affair kept some of them, at least, on the move. Yet it was hard to believe that Clauson and Poinsett were dead, that Brokow had vanished, that Lee Goff was gone. For alone of the group, Goff had told Fessenden he was leaving. He had not needed to tell him why.

Behind him rode the Mixus boys, somber with disappointment at the failure of the attack. They had no qualms about killing, and no lines to draw even at the killing of women. They were in no true sense fighting men; they were butchers. Yet even they realized the change that had come over the group. What had become of Brokow or Goff they did not know. But they did know that disintegration had set in. In turn, these men had turned into a snarling pack of wolves venting their fury and their hatred on each other.

Mustang lay quiet when they rode into town. It was the quiet before the storm. The town, like that cattle buyer who had turned back to Durango, sensed the coming fury of battle. No women were on the street, and only a few hardy souls loitered at the bars or card tables. The chairs before the St. James were deserted, and Clay Allison had ridden back to his home ranch, drunk and ugly.

An almost Sunday peace lay over the sun-swept town when Fessenden drew up before the Mustang Saloon and swung down from his weary horse. Slapping his hat against his leg to beat off the dust, Fessenden stood like a great shaggy bull and surveyed the quiet of the street. He was too knowing a Western man not to recognize the symptoms of disaster. Clapping his hat all awry upon his shaggy head, he shoved his bulk through the doors and moved to the bar.

"Rye," he said, his voice booming in the cavernous interior. His eyes glinted around the room, then back to the bartender.

That worthy could no longer restrain his curiosity. "What's happened?" he asked, swallowing.

A glint of irony came into the hard eyes of the gunman. "Them squatters squatted there for keeps," he said wryly, "an' they showed us they aim to stay put." He tossed off his drink. "All Hades busted loose." Briefly he explained. "You'd a figured there was a thousand men in that neck of the rocks when they opened up. The thing that did it was the unexpectedness of it, like steppin' on a step in the dark when it ain't there."

He poured another drink. "It was that Kedrick," he said grimly. "When I seen him shift to the other side I should've lit a shuck."

"What about Keith?"

"He won't be back."

They turned at the new voice, and saw Dornie Shaw standing in the doorway, smiling. Still smiling, he walked on in and leaned against the bar. "Keith won't be back," he said. "He went for his gun out on Salt Creek."

The news fell into a silent room. A man at a table shifted his feet and his chair creaked. Fessenden wet his lips and downed his second drink. He was getting out of town, but fast.

"Seen that girl come in, short time back," the bartender said suddenly, "that Duane girl. Thought she'd gone over to the other side?"

Dornie's head lifted and his eyes brightened, then shadowed. He downed his own drink and walked jauntily to the door. "Stick around, Fess.

I'll be back." He grinned. "I'll collect for both of us from the Old Man."

The bartender looked at Fessenden. "Reckon he'll bring it if he does?"

The big gunman nodded absently. "Sure. He's no thief. Why, that kid never stole a thing in his life. He don't believe in it. An' he won't lie or swear—but he'll shoot the heart out of you an' smile right in your face while he's doing it."

The show had folded. The roundup was over. There was nothing to do now but light out. Fessenden knew he should go, but a queer apathy had settled over him. He ordered another drink, letting the bartender pour it. The liquor he drank seemed now to fall into a cavern without bottom and had no effect.

On the outskirts of town, Tom Kedrick reined in. "We'll keep together," he said quietly. "We want Keith, Shaw, Burwick, the Mixus boys and Fessenden. There are about four others that you will recognize whom I don't know by name. Let's work fast and make no mistakes.

"Pit, you take Dai and two men and go up the left side of the street. Take no chances. Arrest them if you can. We'll try them, and"—his face was grim —"if we find them guilty they'll have just two sentences: leave the country or hang. The Mixus boys and Shaw," he said, "will hang. They've done murder."

He turned in his saddle and glanced at the tall Texan. "Come on, Shad," he said quietly, "we'll take two men and the right side of the street, which means the livery stable, the St. James and the Mustang."

Kedrick glanced over at Laine. "Pit," he said, "if you run into Allison or Ketchum, better leave 'em alone. We don't want 'em."

Laine's face was grave. "I ain't huntin' 'em," he said grimly, "but if they want it, they can have it."

The parties rode into town and swung down on their respective sides of the street. Laredo grinned at Kedrick, but his eyes were sober. "Nobody wants to cross Laine today," he said quietly. "The man's in a killin' mood. It's his sister."

"Wonder what will happen when they meet?"

"I hope they don't," Shad said. "She's a right purty sort of gal, only money crazy."

The two men stood hesitant, waiting for orders. Both were farmers. One carried a Spencer .56, the other a shotgun. Shad glanced at them. "Let these hombres cover the street, Tom," he suggested. "You take the St. James, an' I'll take the stable."

Kedrick hesitated, "All right," he agreed finally. "But take no chances, boy."

Laredo grinned and waved a negligent hand and walked through the wide door of the stable. Inside, he paused, cold and seemingly careless, actually as poised and deadly as a coiled rattler. He had already seen Abe Mixus' sorrel pony and guessed the two dry-gulchers were in town. He walked on a step and saw the barrel of a rifle push through the hay.

He lunged right and dove into a stall, drawing his gun as he went. He ran full tilt into the other Mixus. Their bodies smashed together, and Mixus, caught off balance, went down and rolled over. He came up, clawing for a gun Laredo kicked the gun from under his hand and sent it spinning into the wide open space between the rows of stalls.

With a kind of whining cry, Bean Mixus sprang after it, slid to his knees and got up, turning. Laredo Shad stood tall and dark, just within the stall. As Mixus turned like a rat cornered and swung his gun around, Laredo Shad fired. His two shots slammed loud in the stillness of the huge barn. Bean Mixus fell dead.

The rifle bellowed and a shot ripped the stall stanchion near Laredo's head. He lunged into the open, firing twice more at the stack of straw. The rifle jerked, then thundered again, but the shot went wild. Laredo dove under the loft where Abe Mixus was concealed, and fired two more shots through the roof over his head where he guessed the killer would be lying.

Switching his guns, he holstered the empty one and waited. The roof creaked some distance away. Laredo began to stalk the escaping Mixus, slipping from stall to stall. Suddenly, a back door creaked and a broad path of light shot into the darkness of the stable. Laredo lunged to follow—too late.

The farmer outside with the shotgun was the man Sloan. As Abe Mixus lunged through the door to escape, they came face to face, at no more than twenty feet of distance. Abe had his rifle at his hip and he fired. The shot ripped through the water trough beside Sloan, and the farmer squeezed off the left-hand barrel of his shotgun.

The solid core of shot hit Mixus in the shoulder and neck, knocking him back against the side of the door. His long face was drawn and terror stricken, his neck and shoulder a mass of blood that seemed to well from a huge wound He fought to get his gun up, Sloan stepped forward, remembering Bob McLennon's death and the deaths of

Steelman and Slagle. The other barrel thundered and a sharp blast of flame stabbed at Abe Mixus.

Smashed and dead, the killer sagged against the doorjamb, his old hat falling free, his face pillowed in the gray, blood-mixed dust.

Silence hung heavy in the wake of the shots. Into that silence Laredo Shad spoke. "Hold it, Sloan!" He stepped through the door, taking no glance at the fallen man. "The other one won't hang, either," he said. "They were both inside."

The two men drew aside, Sloan's face gray and sick. He had never killed a man before, and wanted never to again. He tried to roll a smoke but his fingers trembled. Shad took the paper and tobacco from him and rolled it. The farmer looked up, shame-faced. "Guess I'm yaller," he said. "That sort of got me."

The Texan looked at him gloomily. "Let's hope it always does," he said. He handed him the cigarette. "Try this," he told him. "It will make you feel better. Wonder how Kedrick's comin'?"

"Ain't heard nothin'!"

Pit Laine stood in a door across the street. "Everythin' all right?" he called.

"Yeah," the other farmer called back, "on'y you don't hafta look for the Mixus boys no more. They ain't gonna be around."

Captain Tom Kedrick had walked up the street and turned into the door of the St. James Hotel. The wide lobby was still, a hollow shell, smelling faintly of old tobacco fumes and leather. The wrinkled clerk looked up and shook his head. "Quiet today," he said. "Nobody around. Ain't been no shootin' in days."

Guns thundered from down the street, then again

152

and again. Then there was silence followed by the two solid blasts of the shotgun.

Both men listened, and no further sound came. A moment later Pit Laine called out and the farmer answered. The clerk nodded. "Same town," he said. "Last couple of days I been wonderin' if I wasn't back in Ohio. Awful quiet lately," he said, "awful quiet."

Tom Kedrick walked down the hall and out the back door. He went down the weathered steps and stopped on the grass behind the building. There was an old, rusty pump there, and the sun was hot on the backs of the buildings.

He walked over to the pump and worked the handle. It protested, whining and groaning at the unaccustomed work and finally, despairing of rest, threw up a thick core of water that splashed in the wooden tub. When he had pumped for several minutes, Kedrick held the gourd dipper under the pump and let it fill. The water was clear and very cold. He drank greedily, rested, then drank again.

Far up the backs of the buildings, at the opposite end of town, a man was swinging an ax. Kedrick could see the flash of light on the blade, and see the ax strike home. A moment later, the sound would come to him. He watched, then wiped the back of his hand across his mouth and started along in back of the buildings toward the Mustang.

He moved with extreme care, going steadily, yet with every sense alert. He wore his .44 Russians, and liked the feel of them, ready to his hands. The back door of the Mustang Saloon was long unpainted and blistered by many hot suns. He glanced at the hinges and saw they were rusty. The door

153

would squeak. Then he saw the outside stair leading to the second floor. Turning, he mounted the stairs on tiptoe, easing through the door, and walked down the hall.

In the saloon below, Fessenden had eliminated half a bottle of whisky without destroying the deadening sense of futility that had come over him. He picked up a stack of cards and riffled them skillfully through his fingers. He had not lost his deftness. Whatever effect the whisky had had, it was not on his hands.

Irritated, he slammed the cards down and stared at the bartender. "Wish Dornie'd get back," he said for the tenth time. "I want to leave this town. She don't feel right today."

He had heard the shots down the street, but had not moved from the bar. "Some drunk cowhand," he said irritably.

"You better look," the bartender suggested, hoping for no fights in the saloon. "It might be some of your outfit."

"I got no outfit," Fess replied shortly. "I'm fed up. That stunt out there to Yeller Butte drove me off that range. I'll have no more of it."

He heard the footsteps coming down the hall from upstairs and listened to their even cadence. He glanced up, grinning, "Sounds like an army man. Listen!"

Realization of what he had said came over him, and the grin left his face. He straightened, resting his palms on the bar. For a long moment, he stared into the bartender's eyes. "I knew it! I knew that hombre would—" He tossed off his drink. "Aw, I didn't want to leave town, anyway!"

He turned, moving back from the bar. He stood

straddle legged like a huge grizzly, his big hands swinging at his hips, his eyes glinting upward at the balcony and the hall that gave onto it. The steps ceased, and Tom Kedrick stood there, staring down at him.

Neither man spoke for a full minute, while suspense gripped the watchers, and then it was Fessenden who broke the silence. "You lookin' for me, Kedrick?"

"For any of your crowd. Where's Shaw? And Keith?"

"Keith's dead. Shaw killed him back up on the Salt after you whipped us in the canyon. I dunno where he is now."

Silence fell once more and the two men studied each other. "You were among them at Chimney Rock, Fessenden," Kedrick said. "That was an ambush—dry-gulcher's stunt, Fess." Kedrick took another step forward, then side-stepped down the first step of the stairs which ran along the back wall until about six steps from the bottom, then after a landing, came down facing the room.

Fessenden stood there, swaying slightly on his thick, muscular legs, his brutal jaw and head thrust forward. "Aw, hell!" he said and grabbed iron.

His guns fairly leaped from their holsters spouting flame. A bullet smashed the top of the newel post at the head of the stairs, then ricocheted into the wall. Another punctured a hole just behind Kedrick's shoulder. Tom Kedrick stepped down another step, then fired. His bullet turned Fessenden, and Kedrick ran lightly down four steps while Fessenden smashed two shots at him.

Kedrick dove headlong for the landing, brought up hard against the wall, and smashed another

155

shot at the big man. It knocked a leg from under him and Fessenden rolled over on his feet, colliding with the bar.

He had been hit twice, but he was cold sober and deadly. He braced himself and with his left hand clinging to the bar, lifted his right and thumbed back the hammer. Kedrick fired two quick shots with his left gun. One ripped a furrow down the bar and hit Fessenden below the breast bone—a jagged tearing piece of metal when it struck.

Fessenden fired again, but the bullet went wild. His sixth shot was fired in desperation as he swung up his left-hand gun, dropping the right into his holster. Taking his time, feeling his life's blood running out of him, he braced himself there and took the gun over into his right hand. He was deliberate and calm. "Pour me a drink," he said.

The bartender, lying flat on his face behind the bar, made no move. Tom Kedrick stood on the edge of the landing now, staring at Fessenden. The big gunman had been hit three times, through the shoulder, the leg and the chest, and he still stood there, gun in hand, ponderous and invulnerable.

The gun came up and Fessenden seemed to lean forward with it. "I wish you was Dornie," he said.

Kedrick triggered. The shot nailed Fessenden through the chest again. The big man took a fast step back, then another. His gun slipped from his hand, and he grabbed a glass from the bar. "Gimme a drink!" he demanded. Blood bubbled at his lips.

Tom Kedrick came down the steps, his gun ready in his hand and walked toward Fessenden. Holding his gun level and low down with his right hand, Kedrick picked up the bottle with his left and filled the empty glass. Then he pulled over another glass and poured one for himself.

Fessenden stared at him. "You're a good man, Kedrick," he said, shaping the words patiently. "I'm a good man, too—on the wrong side."

"I'll drink to that." Kedrick lifted his glass, they clicked them, and Fessenden grinned crookedly over his.

"You watch that Dornie," he advised, "he's rattler—mean." The words stumbled from his mouth and he frowned, lifting the glass. He downed his drink, choked on it, and started to hold out his big hand to Kedrick, then fell flat on his face. Holstering his gun, Tom Kedrick leaned over and gripped the big right hand. Fessenden grinned and died.

CHAPTER XV

CONNIE DUANE had reached Mustang only a short time before the survivors of the fight at Yellow Butte began to arrive. Restless, after the men left to return to the squatters' town, she had begun to think of what lay ahead, of Fred Ransome, and of the impending investigation and of her uncle's part in it.

All his papers as well as many of her own remained under lock in the gray stone house in Mustang. If she was to get her own money back from Burwick, or was to clear any part of the blame from her uncle, she knew those papers would be essential. Mounting her horse she left the camp beyond the rim. Striking the Old Mormon Trail, she headed south. She was on that trail when the sun lifted, and she heard the distant sound of shots.

Turning from the trail she reined her horse into the bed of Salt Creek and rode south, passing the point where only a short time later Loren Keith was to meet his death at the hands of Dornie Shaw. Once in town she believed she would be safe. She doubted if anyone would be left in the gray house unless it was Burwick, and she knew that he rarely left his chair.

Arriving in Mustang, she rode quickly up the street, then cut over behind through the back door and went very quietly. Actually, she need not have bothered, for Alton Burwick was not there. Making her way up the old stairs, she unlocked the door to the apartment she had shared with her uncle, and closed the door behind her.

Nothing seemed to have been disturbed. The blinds were drawn as she had left them and the room was still. A little dust had collected, and the light filtering in around the blinds showed it to her. Going to her trunk, she opened it and got out the iron-bound box in which she carried her own papers. It was intact and showed no evidence of having been tampered with. From the bottom of the trunk she took an old purse in which there were two dozen gold eagles. These she put into the purse she was now carrying.

Among other things she found an old pistol, a huge, cumbersome old thing. This she got out and laid on the table beside her. Then she found a derringer seven shot .22 caliber pistol her father had given her several years before he died, and she put it in the pocket of her dress.

Quickly she went into the next room and began to go through her uncle's desk, working swiftly and surely. Most of his papers were readily available. Apparently nobody had made any effort to go through them, probably believing they contained nothing of consequence or that there would be plenty of time later. She was busy at this when she heard a horse walk by the house and stop near the back steps.

Instantly she stopped what she was doing and stood erect. The window here was partly open and she could hear the saddle creak very gently as whoever it was swung down. Then a spur jingled, and there was a step below, then silence.

"So? It's you."

Startled by the voice, Connie turned. Sue Laine stood behind her, staring with wide eyes. "Yes," Connie replied. "I came for some things of mine. You're Sue, aren't you?"

Without replying to the question, the girl nodded her head toward the window. "Who was that? Did you see?"

"No. It was a man."

"Maybe Loren has come back." Sue studied her, unsmiling. "How are they out there? Are they all right? I mean—did you see Pit?"

"Yes. He's unhappy about you."

Sue Laine flushed, but her chin lifted proudly. "I suppose he is, but what did he expect? That I was going to live all my life out there in that awful desert? I'm sick of it! Sick of it, I tell you!"

Connie smiled. "That's strange. I love it. I love it, and every minute I'm there, I love it more. I'd like to spend my life here, and I believe I will."

"With Tom Kedrick?"

Sue's jealousy flashed in her eyes, yet there was curiosity, too. Connie noticed how the other girl studied her clothes, her face.

"Why—I—where did you ever get that idea?"

"From looking at him. What girl wouldn't want him? Anyway, he's the best of the lot."

"I thought you liked Colonel Keith?"

Sue's face flushed again. "I—I thought I did, too. Only part of it was because Tom Kedrick wouldn't notice me. And because I wanted to get away from here, from the desert. But since then—I guess Pit hates me."

"No brother really hates his sister, I think. He'd be glad to see you back with him."

"You don't know him. If it had been anybody but someone associated with Alton Burwick, why—"

"You mean, you knew Burwick before?"

"Knew him?" Sue stared at her. "Didn't you know? Didn't he tell you? He was our stepfather."

"Alton Burwick?" Connie stared in amazement.

"Yes, and we always suspected that he killed my father. We never knew, but my mother suspected later, too, for she took us and ran away from him. He came after us. We never knew what happened to mother. She went off one night for something and never came back, and we were reared by a family who took us in."

A board creaked in the hall, and both girls were suddenly still, listening.

Guns thundered from the street of the town, and both girls stared at each other, holding their breath. There was a brief silence, then a further spattering of shots. Then the door opened very gently and Dornie Shaw stood there facing the two girls.

He seemed startled at finding the girls together and looked from one to the other, his brown eyes bright, but now confused.

Then he centered his eyes on Sue Laine. "You better get out," he said. "Keith's dead."

"Dead?" Sue gasped, horrified. "They—they killed him?"

"No, I did. Up on the Salt. He drew on me."

"Keith—dead." Sue was shocked.

"What about the others? Where are they?" Connie asked quickly.

Dornie turned his head sharply around and looked hard at her, a curious, prying gaze as if he did not quite know what to make of her. "Some of 'em dead," he said matter of factly. "They whupped us. It was that Kedrick," he spoke without emotion or shadow of prejudice as though he were completely indifferent. "He had 'em set for us an' they mowed us down." He jerked his head toward the street. "I guess they are finishin' up now. The Mixus boys an' Fessenden are down there."

"They'll be coming here," Connie said, with conviction. "This is the next place."

"I reckon." He seemed indifferent to that, too. "Kedrick'll be the first one. Maybe," he smiled, "the last one."

He dug out the makings, glancing around the room, then back at Sue. "You git out. I want to talk to Connie."

161

Sue did not move. "You can talk to us both. I like it here."

As he touched his tongue to the paper his eyes lifted and met hers. They were flat, expressionless. "You heard me," he said. "I'd hate to treat you rough."

"You haven't the nerve!" Sue flashed back. "You know what would happen to you if you laid hands on a woman in this country! You can get away with killing me. But this country won't stand for having their women bothered—even by a ratty little killer like you!"

Connie Duane was remembering the derringer in her pocket. She lowered her hand to her hip within easy grasp of the gun.

A sudden cannonade sounded, then a scattering of more shots. At that moment Kedrick was finally shooting it out with Fessenden. Dornie Shaw cocked an inquisitive ear toward the sound. "Gettin' closer," he said. "I ain't really in no hurry until Kedrick gets here."

"You'd better be gone before he does come." Connie was surprised at the confidence in her voice. "He's too much for you, and he's not half frightened like these others are. He'll kill you, Dornie."

He stared at her, then chuckled without humor. "Him? Bah! The man doesn't live who can outdraw Dornie Shaw. I've tried 'em all. Fess? He's supposed to be good, but he don't fool with Dornie. I'd shoot his ears off."

Calmly, Connie dropped her right hand into her pocket and clutched the derringer. The feel of it gave her confidence. "You had better go," she said quietly. "You were not invited here, and we don't want you."

162

He did not move. "Still playin' it high an' mighty, are you? You've got to get over that. Come on, you're coming with me."

"Are you leaving?" Connie's eyes flashed. "I'll not ask you again!"

Shaw started to speak, but whatever it was he planned to say never formed into words, for Connie had her hand on the derringer, and she fired from her pocket. Ordinarily, she was a good shot, but had never fired the gun from that position. The first bullet burned a furrow along Dornie Shaw's ear, notching it at the top. The second shot stung him along the ribs and the third plowed into the table beside him.

With a grunt of surprise, he dove through the door into the hall. Sue was staring at Connie. "Well, I never!" Her eyes dropped to the tiny gun that Connie had now drawn from her pocket. "Dornie Shaw! And with that! Oh, just wait until this gets around!" Her laughter rang out merrily, and despite herself, Connie was laughing, too.

Downstairs near the door, Dornie Shaw clutched his bloody ear. He panted as though he had been running, his face twisting as he stared at his blood. Amazed, he scarcely noticed when Kedrick came up the steps. But as the door pushed open, he saw him. For a fatal instant, he froze. Then he grabbed for his gun, but he had lost his chance. In that split second of hesitation, Kedrick jumped. His right hand grasped Dornie's gun wrist, and Kedrick swung the gunman bodily around, hurling him into the wall. Shaw's body hit with a crash and he rebounded into a wicked right to the wind.

Shaw was no fighter with his hands, and the power of that blow would have wrecked many a bigger man. As it was, it knocked every bit of wind from the gunman's body. Kedrick shoved him back against the wall. "You asked me what I'd do, once, with a faster man. Watch this, Dornie!"

Kedrick lifted his right hand and slapped the gunman across the mouth. Crying with fury, Shaw fought against the bigger man's grip. Kedrick held him flat against the wall, gripping him by the shirt collar, and slapped him over and back. "Just a cheap killer!" Kedrick said calmly. "Somebody has already bled you a little. I'll do it for good."

He dropped a hand to Dornie's shirt and ripped it wide. "I'm going to ruin you in this country, Dornie. I'm going to show them what you are—a cheap, yellow-bellied killer who terrorizes men better than himself." He slapped Dornie again, then shoved him into the wall once more and stepped back.

"All right, Shaw! You got your guns! Reach!"

Almost crying with fury, Dornie Shaw grabbed for his guns. As he whipped them free, all his timing wrecked by the events of the past few minutes, Kedrick's gun crashed and Shaw's right-hand gun was smashed from his hand. Shaw fired the left-hand gun, but the shot went wild. Kedrick lunged, chopping down with his pistol barrel. The blow smashed Dornie Shaw's wrist and he dropped the gun with a yelp.

He fell back against the wall, trembling, and staring at his hands. His left wrist was broken; his right thumb was gone. Where it had been, blood was welling.

Roughly, Kedrick grabbed him and shoved him out of the door. He stumbled and fell, but Kedrick jerked him to his feet, unmindful of the gasps

164

of the onlookers, attracted by the sounds of fighting. In the forefront of the crowd were Pit Laine, Dai Reid and Laredo Shad, blinking with astonishment at the sight of the most feared gunman in the country treated like a whipped child.

Shaw's horse stood nearby, and Kedrick motioned to him. "Get on him—backwards!"

Shaw started to turn and Kedrick lifted his hand and the gunman ducked instinctively. "Get up there! Dai, when he's up tie his ankles together."

Dornie Shaw, befuddled by the whipping he had taken, scarcely aware of what was happening, lifted his eyes. Then he saw the grulla tied near the stone house. It was the last straw, his demoralization was complete.

Feared because of his deadly skill with guns and his love of killing for the sake of killing, he had walked a path alone, either avoided by all, or catered to by them. Never in his life had he been manhandled as he had by Tom Kedrick. His belief in himself was shattered.

"Take him through the town." Kedrick's voice was harsh. "Show them what a killer looks like. Then fix up that thumb and wrist and turn him loose."

"Turn him loose?" Shad demanded. "Are you crazy?"

"No, turn him loose. He'll leave this country so far behind nobody will ever see him again. This is worse than death for him, believe me." He shrugged. "I've seen them before. All they need, that kind, is for somebody to face them once who isn't afraid. He was fast and accurate with his guns so he developed the idea he was tough.

"Other folks thought the same thing. He wasn't tough. A tough man has to win and lose. He has to

165

come up after being knocked down, he has to have taken a few beatings, and know what it means to win the hard way.

"Anybody," he said dryly, "can knock a man down. When you've been knocked down at least three times yourself, and then got up and floored the other man, then you can figure you're a tough hombre. Those smoke poles of Shaw's greased his path for him. Now he knows what he's worth."

The crowd drifted away and Connie Duane was standing in the doorway. Tom Kedrick looked up at her, and suddenly, he smiled. To see her now, standing like this in the doorway, was like life-giving rain upon the desert, coming in the wake of many heat-filled days.

She came down the step to him, then looked past him at Pit. "Your sister's upstairs, Pit. You'd better talk to her."

Laine hesitated; then he said stiffly, "I don't reckon I want to."

Laredo Shad drew deep on his cigarette and squinted through the smoke at Laine. "Mind if I do?" he asked. "I like her."

Pit Laine was astonished. "After this?"

Shad looked at the fire end of his cigarette. "Well," he said, speaking seriously, "the best cuttin' horse I ever rode was the hardest to break. Them with lots of git up an' go to 'em often make the best stock."

"Then go ahead." Pit stared after him. Then he said, "Tell her I'll be along later."

CHAPTER XVI

FOR three weeks there was no sign of Alton Burwick. He seemed to have vanished into the earth, and riders around the country reported no sign of him.

At the end of that time three men got down from the afternoon stage and were shown to rooms in the St. James. An hour later, while they were at dinner, Captain Tom Kedrick pushed open the door and walked into the dining room. Insfantly, one of the men, a tall, immaculate young man whose hair was turning gray at the temples, rose to meet him, hand outstretched. "Tom! Say, this is wonderful! Gentlemen, this is Tom Kedrick, the man I was telling you about. We served together in the War Between the States! Tom—Mr. Edgerton and Mr. Cummings."

The two men, one a pudgy man with a round, cheerful face, the other as tall as Frederic Ransome and with gray muttonchop whiskers acknowledged the introduction. When Kedrick had seated himself, they began demanding details. Quietly, and as concisely as possible, he told them his own story, be-

167

ginning with his joining the company in New Orleans.

"And Burwick's gone?" Edgerton asked. He was the older man with the muttonchop whiskers. "Was he killed?"

"I doubt it, sir," Kedrick replied. "He simply vanished. The man had a faculty for being out of the way when trouble came. Since he left, with the aid of Miss Duane and her uncle's papers, we managed to put together most of the facts. However, Burwick's papers have disappeared, or most of them."

"Disappeared?" Edgerton asked. "How did that happen?"

"Miss Duane tells me that when she entered the house before the final trouble with Shaw, she passed the office door and the place was undisturbed and the desk all in order. After the crowd had gone and when we returned, somebody had been rifling the desk and the safe."

"You imply that Burwick returned? That he was there then?"

"He must have been. Connie—Miss Duane—tells me that only he had the combination, and that he kept all the loose ends of the business in his hands."

Cummings stared hard at Kedrick. "You say this, this Shaw fellow killed Keith? How do we know that you didn't? You admit to killing Fessenden."

"I did kill him. In a fair fight before witnesses. I never even saw Keith's body after he was killed."

"Who do you think killed John Gunter?" Cummings demanded.

"My guess would be Burwick."

"I'm glad you're not accusing Keith of that," Cummings replied dryly.

"Keith wouldn't have used a knife," Kedrick replied quietly, "nor he wouldn't have attacked him from behind as was obviously the case."

"This land deal, Kedrick," Ransome asked. "Where do you stand in it?"

"I? I don't stand at all. I'm simply not in it."

Cummings looked up sharply. "You don't stand to profit from it at all? Not in any way?"

"How could I? I own nothing. I have no holdings, nor claim to any."

"You said Burwick promised you fifteen per cent?"

"That's right. But I know now that it was merely to appease me long enough to get me on the spot at Chimney Butte where I was to be killed along with the others. Burwick got me there, then rode off on the pretext that he wanted to look at a mineral ledge."

"How about this girl? The Duane girl?" Cummings asked sharply. "Does she stand to profit?"

"She will be fortunate to get back her money that her uncle invested."

"See, Cummings?" Ransome said. "I told you Kedrick was honest. I know the man."

"I'll give my opinion on that later, after this investigation is completed. Not now. I want to go over the ground and look into this matter thoroughly. I want to investigate this matter of the disappearance of Alton Burwick, too. I'm not at all satisfied with this situation."

He glanced down at the notes in his hand, then looked up "As to that, Kedrick, wasn't Fessenden a duly elected officer of the law when you shot him? Wasn't he the sheriff?"

"Elected by a kangaroo election," Kedrick replied, "where the votes were counted by the two officials who won. If that is a legal election, then he was sheriff."

"I see. But you do not deny that he had authority?"

"I do deny it."

Connie Duane was awaiting him when he walked back to his table. She smiled as he sat down and listened to his explanation. She frowned thoughtfully. "Cummings? I think there is something in Uncle John's papers about him. I believe he was acting for them in Washington."

"That explains a lot then." Kedrick picked up his coffee cup, then put it down abruptly, for Laredo Shad had come into the room, his face sharp and serious. He glanced around, and sighting Kedrick, hurried toward him, spurs jingling. Kedrick got to his feet. "What's wrong? What's happened?"

"Plenty! Sloan was wounded last night and Yellow Butte burned!"

"What?" Kedrick stared.

Shad nodded grimly. "You shouldn't have turned that rat loose. That Dornie Shaw."

Kedrick shook his head irritably. "I don't believe it. He was thoroughly whipped when he left here. I think he ran like a scared rabbit when he left. If he did want revenge, it would be after a few months, not so soon. No, this is somebody else."

"Who could it be?"

His eyes met Connie's and she nodded, her eyes frightened. "You know who it could be, Tom. It could be Burwick."

Of course, that was what he had been thinking. Burwick had bothered him, getting away scot free, dropping off the end of the world into oblivion as he had. Remembering the malignant look in the man's eyes, Kedrick—was even more positive. Burwick had counted on this land deal; he had worked on it longer than any one of them, and it meant more to him.

"Shad," he said suddenly, "where does that grulla tie in? It keeps turning up, again and again. There's something more about all this than we've ever known, something that goes a lot deeper. Who rides the grulla? Why is it he has never been seen? Why was Dornie so afraid of it?"

"Was he afraid of the grulla?" Shad asked, frowning. "That doesn't figure."

"Why doesn't it? That's the question now. You know, that last day when I had Shaw thoroughly whipped, he looked up and saw something that scared him, yet something that I think he more than half expected. After he was gone down the street, I looked around, and there was nothing there. Later, I stumbled across the tracks of the grulla mustang. That horse was in front of the house during all the excitement!"

Frederic Ransome came into the room again and walked to their table. "Cummings is going to stir up trouble," he said, dropping into a chair. "He's out to get you, Kedrick, and if he can pin the killing of Keith on you, or that of Burwick . . . He claims your story is an elaborate build-up to cover the murder of all three of the company partners. He can make so much trouble that none of the squatters will get anything out of the land, and nothing for all their work. We've got to find Burwick."

Laredo lit a cigarette. "That's a tough one," he said, "but maybe I've got a hunch."

171

"What?" Kedrick looked up.

"Ever hear Burwick talk about the grulla?"

"No, I can't say that I did. It was mentioned before him once that I recall, and he didn't seem interested."

"Maybe he wasn't interested because he knowed all about it," Shad suggested. "That Burwick has me puzzled."

Connie looked up at him. "You may be right, Laredo, but Pit and Sue Laine were Burwick's stepchildren and they knew nothing about the horse. The only one who seemed to know anything was Dornie Shaw."

Tom Kedrick got up. "Well, there's one thing we can do," he said. "Laredo, we can scout out the tracks of that horse and trail it down. Pick up an old trail, anything. Then just see where it takes us."

On the third day it began to rain. All week the wind had been chill and cold and clouds had hung low and flat across the sky from horizon to horizon. Hunched in his slicker, Laredo slapped his gloved hands together and swore. "This finishes it!" he said with disgust. "It will wipe out all the trails for us!"

"All old anyway," Kedrick agreed. "We've followed a dozen here lately, and none of them took us anywhere. All disappeared on rock or were swept away by wind."

"Escavada's cabin isn't far up this canyon," Shad suggested. "Let's hit him up for chow. It will be a chance to get warm, anyway."

"Know him?"

"Stopped in there once. He's half Spanish, half Ute. Tough old blister, an' been in this country since before the grass came. He might be able to tell us something."

The trail into the canyon was slippery and the dull red of the rocks had turned black under the downpour. The rain slanted across the sky in drenching sheets. By the time they reached the stone cabin in the corner of the hills both men and horses were cold, wet and hungry.

Escavada opened the door for them and waved them in. He grinned at them. "Glad to have company," he said. "Ain't seen a man for three weeks."

When they had stripped off their slickers and peeled down to shirts, pants and boots, he put coffee before them and laced it with a strong shot of whisky. "Warm you up," he said. "Trust you ain't goin' out again soon. Whisky's mighty fine when a body comes in from the cold, but not if he's goin' out again. It flushes the skin up, fetches all the heat to the surface, then gives it off into the air. Man freezes mighty quick, drinkin' whisky."

"You ever see a grulla mustang around, Escavada?" Laredo asked suddenly, looking up at the old man.

He turned on them, his eyes bright with malicious humor. "You ain't some of them superstitious kind, be you? Skeered o' the dark like? An' ghosts?"

"No," Kedrick said, "but what's the tie-up?"

"That grulla. Old story in this here country. Dates back thirty, forty years. Maybe further'n that. Sign of death or misfortune, folks say."

Laredo looked inquiringly at Kedrick, and Kedrick asked, "You know anything about it? That horse is real enough. We've both seen the grulla."

"So've I," the old man said. He dropped into a chair and grinned at them. His gray hair was sparse, but his eyes were alive and young. "I seen it many times, an' no misfortune come my way. Not unless you call losin' my shovel a misfortune."

He hitched his chair nearer the woodpile and tossed a couple of sticks on the fire. "First I heerd of it was long ago. Old folks used to tell of a Spanish man in armor ridin' a mouse-colored horse. He used to come an' go about the hills, but the story back of it seems to be that a long time back some such feller was mighty cruel to the Injuns. That story sort of hung around an' a body heerd it ever' now and again until about fifteen, sixteen years back. Since then she's been mighty lively."

"You mean, you heard the story more since then?" Kedrick asked.

"Uh huh. Started with a wagon train wiped out by Injuns up on the Salt. Ever' man jack o' them kilt dead—women folks, too, the story was. There was a youngster come off scot free, boy about five or six years old. He crawled off into the brush, an' after, he swore them Injuns was led by a white man on a grulla horse, a white man in armor!"

"Wild yarn," Shad said, "but you can't blame the kid, imaginin' things after what he must've seen."

"He said that hombre in the armor went around with a long knife, an' he skewered ever' one of the bodies to make sure they was real dead. He said once that hombre looked right square at him, layin' in the brush. He was skeered like all git out, but must've been he wasn't seen, 'cause he wasn't bothered."

"An' this grulla has been seen since?" Shad asked. "Reg'lar?"

"Uh huh, but never no rider clost enough to say who or what. Sometimes off at a distance, sometimes just the horse, standin'. Most folks git clear off when they see that horse."

He got up and brought back the coffee pot. "Right odd you should ast me about him now," he commented. "Right odd."

Both men looked at him, and sensing their acute interest, he continued. "Been huntin' here lately. Some days back I ketched me a few bees off the cactus an' mesquite, figurin' to start a bee line. Well, I got her started, all right, an' I trailed them bees to a place far south o' here.

"South an' west, actually. Most o' this country hereabouts is worked out o' bees. I been at it too long, so I was workin' a good ways off. Well, my bee line took me over toward the Hogback. You know that place?

"She's a high curvin' ridge maybe five or six hundred feet at the crest, but she rises mighty close to straight up for four hundred feet. Crawlin' up there to locate the cave them bees was workin' out of, I come on a cave like a cliff dwellin', on'y it wasn't. She was man-made, an' most likely in the past twenty years or so.

"What started me really lookin' was my shovel—the one I lost. She was right there on that ledge, so I knowed it hadn't been lost, but stole off me. I began huntin' around. I found back inside this place it was all fixed up for livin'. Some grub there, blankets, a couple of guns, an' under some duffle in the corner, an old-time breastplate an' helmet."

"You're serious?" Kedrick demanded incredulously.

"Sure as I'm alive! But," Escavada chuckled, "that ain't the best of it. Lyin' there on the floor, deader'n last year's hopes, was a young feller. He had a knife, old-time Spanish knife that a feller in armor might

175

have carried, an' it was skewered right th'ough him!"

"A young man—dead?" Kedrick suddenly leaned forward. "Anything odd about him? I mean, was he missing a thumb?"

Escavada stared. "Well now, if that don't beat all! He was missin' a thumb, an' he was crippled up mighty bad in the other arm. Carried her in a sling."

"Dornie Shaw!" Laredo leaped to his feet. "Dornie Shaw, by all that's holy!"

"Shaw?" Escavada puckered his brows, his old eyes gleaming. "Now that's most odd, most odd. Shaw was the name o' that boy, the one who didn't git killed with the wagon train!"

Kedrick's face was a study. Dornie Shaw—dead! But if Dornie had been the boy from the wagon train, that would account for his superstitious fear of the grulla mustang. But to suppose that after all these years Dornie had been killed by the same man, or ghost if one believed in ghosts, that killed the rest of them so many years before was too ridiculous. It was, he thought suddenly, unless you look at it just one way.

"Man can't escape his fate," Escavada said gloomily. "That boy hid out from that knife, but in the end it got him."

Kedrick got up. "Could you take us to that place, Escavada? Down there on the Hogback?"

"I reckon." He glanced outside. "But not in this rain. Rheumatiz gits me."

"Then tell me where it is," Kedrick said, "because I'm going now!"

They were crossing the head of Coal Mine Creek

when Laredo saw the tracks. He drew up suddenly, pointing. The tracks of a horse, well shod. "The grulla!" Kedrick said grimly. "I'd know those tracks anywhere!"

They pushed on. It was very late, and the pelting rain still poured down upon their heads and shoulders. The trails were slippery, and dusk was near. "We'd better find us a hole to crawl into," Shad suggested. We'll never find that horse in this weather!"

"By morning the tracks will be gone, and I've a hunch we'll find our man right in that cliff dwelling where Escavada saw Dornie's body!"

"Wonder how Dornie found the place?"

"If what I think is right," Kedrick replied, wiping the rain from his face, "he must have run into an old friend and been taken there to hide out. That old friend was the same rider of the grulla that killed his family and friends with the wagon train, and when he saw that armor, he knew it."

"But what's it all about?" Shad grumbled. "It don't make sense! An' no horse lives that long."

"Sure not. There may have been a half-dozen grullas in that length of time. This man probably tried to capitalize on the fears of the Indians and Mexicans who live up that way to keep them off his trail. We'll probably find the answer when we reach the end of our ride."

The Hogback loomed black and ominous before them. The trail, partly switchback and part sheer climb, led over the sharp, knifelike ridge. They mounted, their horses laboring heavily at the steep and slippery climb. Twice Tom Kedrick saw the tracks of the grulla on the trail, and in neither case could those tracks have been more than an hour old.

Kedrick glanced down when they saw the opposite side, then dismounted. "This one is tricky,"
he said grimly. "We'd better walk it."

Halfway down, lightning flashed, and in the
momentary brightness, Laredo called out, "Watch
it, Tom! High, right!"

Kedrick's head jerked around just as the rifle
boomed. The bullet smacked viciously against the
rock beside him, spattering his face with splinters.
He grabbed for his gun, but it was under his slicker. The gun boomed again, five fast shots, as fast
as the marksman could work the lever of his rifle.

Behind Tom Kedrick the anguished scream of a
wounded horse cut the night, and Shad's warning
yell was drowned in the boom of the gun again.
Then he flattened against the rock barely in time
to avoid the plunging, screaming horse.

His own appaloosa, frightened, darted down the
trail with the agility of a mountain goat. The rifle
boomed again and Kedrick dropped flat.

"Shad? You all right?"

There was a moment before the reply, then it
was hoarse, but calm. "Winged me, but not bad."

"I'm going after him. You all right?"

"Yeah. You might help me wrap this leg up."

Sheltered by the glistening, rain-wet rock, with
gray mist swirling past them on the high ridge of
the Hogback, Kedrick knelt in the rain. Shielding the
bandage from the rain with a slicker, he bound
the leg. The bullet had torn through the flesh, but
the bone was not broken.

CHAPTER XVII

WHEN the wound was bandaged, Kedrick drew back into the shelter of the slight overhang and stared about. Ahead and below them was a sea of inky blackness. Somewhere down that mountain would be their horses, one probably dead or dying, the other possibly crippled.

Around them all was night and the high, windy, rain-wet rocks. And out there in the darkness a killer stalked them—a killer, who could at all of three hundred yards, spot his shots so well as to score two hits on a target seen only by a brief flash of lightning. Next time those shots could kill. And there was no doubt about it. Now the situation was clear. It was kill or be killed.

"Sure," Laredo said dryly, "you got to get him, man. But you watch it. He's no slouch with that Spencer!"

"You've got to get off this ridge," Kedrick insisted, "the cold and rain up here will kill you!"

"You leave that to me," Shad replied shortly. "I'll drag myself down the trail an' find a hole to crawl into down on the flat below this Hogback. Might even find your palouse down there. You got grub an' coffee in those saddle bags?"

"Yeah, but you'd better not try a fire until I come back."

Shad chuckled. "Make sure you come back. I never did like to eat alone."

Slipping his hands under his slicker through the pockets, Tom gripped his guns. His rifle, of course, was in his saddle scabbard. He was going to have to stalk a skilled killer—a fine marksman who was on his own ground—in absolute darkness with a hand gun. And the killer had a Spencer .56!

Lightning flashed, but there was no more shooting. Somewhere out there the killer was stalking them. He would not give up now, nor retreat. This, for him, was a last stand unless he killed them both. His hideout now was known, and if they escaped he would no longer be safe. That he did not intend to be driven from the country was already obvious by the fact that he had stayed this long.

Kedrick crawled out, using a bush to cover his movement. Working along the windy top of the ridge, he moved toward a nest of boulders he had seen ahead of him by the lightning flash. The wind whipped at his hat and flapped the skirt of his slicker. His right hand gun was drawn, but under the slicker.

He crawled on. Lightning flashed and he flattened out on the rocks. But the Spencer bellowed, the bullet smashing his eyes and mouth full of gravel. Rolling over, he held his fire, spitting and pawing desperately at his blinded eyes.

There was no sound but the wind and rain. Then in the distance, thunder roared and rumbled off among the peaks. When the lightning flashed again, he looked out along the high ridge of the Hogback.

Lashed by the driving rain, its rocks glistened like steel under clouds that seemed a scarce arm's length above Kedrick's head. Mist drifted by him, touching his wet face with a ghostly hand, and the weird white skeletons of long dead pines pointed their sharp and bony fingers toward the sky.

Rain pelted against his face, and he cowered, fearing the strike of a bullet at each flash of lightning, smelling the brimstone as the lightning scarred the high ridge with darting flame. He touched his lips with his tongue and stared until his eyes ached with strain.

His mouth was dry and his stomach empty, and something mounted within him. Fear? Panic? He could stay still no longer. With infinite patience, he edged forward, working his way a little over the edge of the ridge toward the hulking black clumps of some juniper, ragged trees, whipped to agonized shapes by generations of wind.

There was no sound but the storm, no sight of anything. He moved on, trying to estimate how far away the cliff house would be, to guess if he could reach it first or get between it and the killer out there. Flame stabbed the night and something burned sharply along his shoulders. He let go everything and rolled, went crashing down a dozen feet before he brought up in a tangle of dead limbs.

But the killer was not waiting. Suddenly he loomed dark on the crest. Crouching like a hunted animal, every instinct alert, Kedrick fired.

The dark figure jerked hard, and then the Spencer bellowed. The bullet plastered a branch near Kedrick, and he knew that only his own shot had saved his life. He fired again, and then deliberately hurled himself backward into the night, falling, landing, crawling. He got to his feet and plunged into the absolute darkness, risking a broken limb or a bad fall—anything to get the distance he needed. Then lightning flashed, and as if by magic the Spencer boomed. How the man had followed his plunging career he could not know, but he felt the stab and slam of the bullets as they smashed about him. This man was shooting too close. He couldn't miss long!

His shoulders burned, but whether that shot had been a real wound or a mere graze he did not know. Something fluid trickled down his spine. But whether it was rain water through the slit coat or his own blood, he could not guess.

He moved back, circling. Another shot, but this slightly to his left. Quickly he moved left and a shot smacked right near where he had been standing. The killer was using searching fire now, and he was getting closer.

Kedrick moved back, tripped and fell, and bullets laced the air over him. Evidently the man had a belt full of ammunition, or his pockets were stuffed.

Kedrick started to rise. This time his fingers found the hard smoothness not of rock, but of earth and gravel. Carefully, he felt about in the darkness.

The path! He was on a path, and no doubt the path to the cliff house.

He began to move along it, feeling his way carefully. Once, off to his left, he heard a rock roll. He took a chance and fired blind, then rolled over three times and felt the air split apart as the shots slammed the ground where he had been. He fired again, then again, always moving.

Lightning flashed, and he saw a hulking thing back on the trail the way he had come, a huge, glistening thing, black and shining. Flame sprang from it, and he felt the shock of the bullet, then steadied himself and fired again.

Deliberately then, he turned and worked his way down the path. Suddenly, he felt space before him, and found the path here took a sharp turn. Another step and he might have plunged off! How near was his escape he knew in another instant when lightning flashed and he saw far below him the gray-white figure of the appaloosa standing in the rain.

He worked his way down the cliff, then found a ledge and in a moment, his hands found the crude stone bricks of the cliff house. Feeling his way along it, he felt for the door, and then pushing it open he crawled into the inner darkness and pushed the door shut behind him.

After the lashing of wind and rain the peace seemed a miracle. Jerking off his soaking hat he tossed it aside, and threw off the slicker. There was a chance the killer would not guess that he knew of this place. Undoubtedly had Kedrick not known of it he would have passed it by in the darkness and storm.

Working his way along the floor he found a curtain dividing the first chamber from an inner room. He stepped through it and sat down hard on the bunk. Feeling for his left-hand gun he found the holster empty, and he had fired five shots with his right gun Suddenly, the curtain stirred and there was a breath of wind Then it vanished. The killer was in the other room. He had come in.

Kedrick dared not rise for fear the bed would

creak. He heard a match strike, and then a candle was lighted. Feet shuffled in the other room. Then a voice. "I know you're in there, Kedrick. There's water on the floor in here. I'm behind a piece of old stone wall that I use for a sort of table. I'm safe from your fire. I know there's no protection where you are. Throw your guns out and come with your hands up! If you don't, I'm going to open fire an' search every inch of that room!"

Over the top of the blanket curtain which was suspended from a pole across the door, Tom Kedrick could see the roof in the other room. The cave house was actually much higher than need be. Evidently the killer had walled up an overhang or cave. Kedrick could see several heavy cedar beams that had served to support a ceiling now mostly gone. If that was true in the other room, it might be true in his also.

He straightened to his feet. He heard a sudden move and then fired.

From the other room came a chuckle. "Figured that would draw fire! Well, one gun's empty. Now toss out the other an' come out. You haven't a chance!"

Kedrick did not reply. He was reaching up into the darkness over his head, feeling for the beams. He touched one, barely touched it, then reached up with both hands. He judged the distance he had to jump by the width of the beams in the other room.

What if it were old and would not support his weight? He had to chance that.

He jumped, his fingers hooked well over the edge and, soundlessly, he drew himself up. Now, Kedrick could see into the lighted room, but he could not locate the killer. The voice spoke again. "I'm giving you no more time, Kedrick. Come out or I start to shoot! Toss that other gun first!"

Silence lay in the room, a silence broken by the sudden bellow of a gun. The killer fired, emptied a six-gun, then emptied another. Tom Kedrick waited, having no idea how many guns the man had, or what he might have planned for. Then six more carefully spaced shots were fired. One of them ricocheting dangerously close to Kedrick's head.

A long pause, and then a sound of movement. "All right, if you're alive in there now, you got a shot comin' but if you want to give up, you can. I sort of want you alive."

Suddenly the blanket was jerked from its moorings and Alton Burwick stood in the opening, a gun gripped in his fist, ready to fire.

Kedrick made no sound, and the man stared, then rushed into the room. Almost whining with fury, he jerked Kedrick's hat from the bed, then the slicker. As the latter fell to the floor, with it fell Kedrick's other pistol, which falling from the holster had hooked into some tear in the slicker. He stared at it furiously, and then jerked the bed aside. Almost insane with anger, he searched, unbelieving and whining like an angry hound on a trail.

He stopped, his pent-up fury worn away and stood there, his chest heaving with his exertions, his fist still gripping the pistol. "Gone! Gone!" he cried, as if bereft. "When I had him right here!"

Kedrick's fingers had found a tiny sliver of wood, and, deliberately, he snapped it against Burwick's cheek. The fat man jerked as if stung, then looked up. Their eyes met, and slowly he backed away, but now he was smiling. "Oh, you're a smart one, Kedrick. Very smart! Too bad it couldn't have been you with me instead of that weakling Keith. All front and show, but no bottom to him, no staying quality!

"But," he sighed, "I've got you anyway, and you'll suffer for what you've done." He scooped Kedrick's other pistol from the floor and backed away. "All right, get down!"

Kedrick dropped to the floor, and the fat man waved irritably at the gun he clutched. "No use to bluff. That's empty. Throw it down!"

"What's it all about, Burwick?" Tom asked suddenly. "Why this place? The armor? What about Dornie Shaw?"

"Ah? How did you know about that? But no matter, no matter." He backed to the wall, watching Kedrick and holding the gun. "Why, it was gold, boy! Gold, and lots of it! It was I who stirred those Indians up to attacking that caravan! I wanted the gold they carried, and most of it belonging to Dornie's pal!

"I knew about it! Followed them from Dodge. Knew when they drew it from the bank there, and how much!

"They fooled me though. When the Indians hit, they'd buried it somewhere. It could have been a lot of places, that was the trouble. They might have buried it sooner, but somewhere along the trail. I've dug and I've hunted, but I've never found it. Maybe I will someday—but nobody else is going to!

"Wondered why I wanted the land? Profit, sure!

186

But I wanted this piece, a couple of sections in here, all for myself. Figured on that, working it out somehow. The gold's somewhere between here and Thieving Rock. Has to be."

Kedrick nodded. "That clears up a lot of things. Now you drop that gun, Burwick, and come as my prisoner."

Burwick chuckled fatly. "Try to bluff me? I'd of expected that from you! Nervy one, huh? Bet you got that Connie Duane, too! By the Lord Harry, there's a woman! No scare to her. Not one bit! Drop your gun, boy, or I'll put my first bullet through your knee cap!"

He was going to shoot, and Tom Kedrick knew it. Coolly, he squeezed off his own shot, an instant faster. He shot for the gun hand, but the bullet only skinned the thumb knuckle and hit Burwick in the side.

The fat man jerked and his face twisted, and he stared at the gun, lifting his own. Coolly, Kedrick fired again, then again. The bullets struck with an ugly smack, and Burwick wilted, the gun going from his limp fingers to the floor. Kedrick stepped in and caught him, easing him down. The flabby cheeks were suddenly sagging and old. Bitterly, the man stared upward at him. "What happened? That—that—?"

"The gun was a Walch twelve-shot Navy pistol," Tom explained. "I started carrying them a few days ago, replacing the .44 Russians."

Burwick stared at him, no hatred in his eyes. "Smart!" he said. "Smart! Always one trick better than me, or anybody! You'll—do, boy!"

On the streets of Mustang the sun was warm after

the rain. Tom Kedrick, wounded again but walking, stood beside Connie Duane. Shad was grinning at them. "Look mighty fine in that tailored suit, Tom. You goin' to be gone long?"

"Not us! We'll be married in Santa Fe, and then we're headin' for the Mogollons and that ranch."

"Seems a shame not to hunt for that gold," Laredo complained. "But anyway, the real treasure was that box full of Burwick's papers. Sure made Cummings hunt his hole. But I do regret that gold."

"I don't," Connie replied, "it's caused too much trouble. Alton Burwick spent his life and a good many other lives after it. Let it stay where it is. Maybe a better man will find it, one who needs it more than we do."

"Gosh!" Laredo said suddenly. "I got to light a shuck! I'm late to meet Sue! So long, then!" They watched him go, waiting for the stage.

Everything was quiet in Mustang—three whole days without a killing.

The Legends of the Old West
Live On in Fawcett Westerns

☐ BUCHANAN'S BIG FIGHT by Jonas Ward	14406	$1.95
☐ TRACKDOWN by Dean Owen	04644	$1.95
☐ THE UNTAMED BREED by Gordon D. Shirreffs	14387	$2.75
☐ LITTLE BIG MAN by Thomas Berger	23854	$2.95
☐ HONDO by Louis L'Amour	14255	$2.25
☐ HE RODE ALONE by Steve Frazee	14103	$1.75
☐ SWEENY'S HONOR by Brian Garfield	24330	$1.95
☐ RETURN TO ARAPAHOE by Charles N. Heckelmann	04590	$1.75
☐ CROSSFIRE TRAIL by Louis L'Amour	14276	$1.95

Buy them at your local bookstore or use this handy coupon for ordering.

COLUMBIA BOOK SERVICE, CBS Publications
32275 Mally Road, P.O. Box FB, Madison Heights, MI 48071

Please send me the books I have checked above. Orders for less than 5 books must include 75¢ for the first book and 25¢ for each additional book to cover postage and handling. Orders for 5 books or more postage is FREE. Send check or money order only.

Cost $_____   Name _____

Sales tax*_____   Address _____

Postage_____   City _____

Total $_____   State _____ Zip _____

* The government requires us to collect sales tax in all states except AK, DE, MT, NH and OR.

This offer expires 1 March 82   8181

GREAT ADVENTURES IN READING

NEW FROM POPULAR LIBRARY

☐ **FALLING IN PLACE**   04650 $2.95
   by Ann Beattie

☐ **THURSDAY'S CHILD**   04656 $2.95
   by Victoria Poole

☐ **RIVIERA**   04657 $2.75
   by Robert Sydney Hopkins

☐ **THE ZERO TRAP**   04660 $2.50
   by Paula Gosling

☐ **FORCE PLAY**   04658 $1.95
   by Anthony Stuart

☐ **KEEPING TIME**   04659 $2.25
   by David Bear